THE BED WE MADE

COAL WADA FRESH

MAJOR KEY
PUBLISHING

I dedicate this book to:
Willie Robert Jr - A true king and head of the family. RIP.
To Laura, Ashanti, Tee Dee, Destiny, Elijah, London, Moses and Hannah. My circle of trust.
To Shaelyn. She has no idea. I'll leave it at that.
To the readers. There are a million different books you could be reading right now, but you chose this one. I am truly grateful. Oh yeah, if I've offended anybody by this story, I apologize. I am not a mainstream writer. I'm Coal Wada Fresh.

PROLOGUE

In the beginning, there were three types of humans: One male, one female, and one that was part male and female. Each human type had four hands, four feet, and one head with two faces. What they lacked in beauty, they made up for in strength and bravery. They even had the audacity to challenge the Gods. Zeus was fed up and decided to split these creatures in half to weaken them while increasing their numbers. His plan was that there would be more humans to offer sacrifices, but they'd be too weak to challenge the Gods. However, with the split, he inadvertently created us. Lonely creatures forever searching for our other halves. Humans were originally one, and we were a whole. The desire and pursuit of the whole is the definition of searching for our soulmates....

ONE

Welcome to the Southside of Montgomery. Home to some of the prettiest women and fast-talking woman-izers you'll ever come across. It was six o'clock on a lazy Sunday afternoon. A strong scent of soul food choked the Regency Park neighborhood like a blunt of high-grade marijuana. YFN Lucci's hit single "Key to The Streets" bumped from an old radio sitting on the bathroom floor while thirteen-year-old Bruno Santana brushed his wavy hair in the mirror. He was just about ready to jump on his Mongoose bike and head over to Looney's Skating Rink like he did every Sunday night with his homeboys for the Sunday Freak Fest. His little sister Bella burst into the bathroom.

"Yo' friends on the porch, Bruno!" she spat with her tiny hands on her boney little hips like a pee wee Army drill sergeant.

"They should be. It's 'bout that time," he answered, looking himself over one last time in the mirror.

He then hurried out of the house to catch up with his homeboys. Mason Monroe, Orlando Hung, and Poncho

Guzman were waiting for him on the front porch. They all wore matching crispy white T-shirts, black Levi jeans, and white Air Force Ones. They'd been best friends since elementary school. It was impossible to see one without the other. They called themselves The Four Locos.

"Damn, hood, let me find out y'all tryna look like me," Bruno said as he bumped the rock with each one of his homies.

"Nah, hood. You know me and Poncho introduced y'all to this world of high hood fashion," Mason responded with a smile as long as Highway 65 stretched across his face.

Mason was always in a good mood even though his family scenario was anything other than a happy environment. His mother was a violent, bitter woman whose addiction was not only drinking large amounts of cheap vodka, but also beating the shit out of her only child. There was numerous nights Mason found himself floating between different family members' houses to escape her drunken fury. But through it all, he never lost the urge to flash those pearly whites to anybody he came in contact with.

"Yeah, Bruno. I remember when you and Orlando was rocking them Wrangler jeans, looking like some straight lames," Poncho joked as he sipped on his Orangeade drink concealed inside a small brown paper bag.

Poncho was an unexpected figure in this Southside tale. He was a full-blooded Mexican, which was unheard of in the Dirty South. But he was raised with the homeboys, so he was what they were; Locos.

"I don't know what these fools talkin' 'bout. I remember when Poncho and Mason were wearing shorts so short and tight that every time they bent down to tie they shoes, niggas was stuffing dollar bills in they boxers," Orlando said, laughing.

Orlando was the Don Juan of the crew. If a girl was born with a pair of working ears on her head, she didn't have a chance of resisting his hypnotic conversation. He was a playa bred down from a long bloodline of pimps and womanizers. If a youngsta had a girlfriend that he wanted to keep, he definitely had to keep her away from Orlando. No ifs, ands, or buts about it.

"I know right. Even to this day, if one of 'em see a dollar bill, they get to shakin' like a stripper," Bruno co-signed.

Bruno was a spoiled, young nigga. His Madear adored him and his six-year-old sister Bella more than anything in this world. She even loved their father; the no good, lying, cheating, backstabbing, deadbeat who hadn't been seen in the last five years. Even though he was a piece of shit, he had blessed his baby mama with two sweet-natured children whom she loved more than God himself. For that reason alone, she would always have a soft spot for him inside of her heart. Bruno loved his Madear to death but didn't share her views. He had no soft spot inside himself for a rolling stone who abandoned him and his baby sister for no apparent reason. But none of that mattered at the moment. The only thing on these young niggas' minds was hanging out and putting their mack down on some bad bitches. So, as they cruised their bikes out of Regency Park on their way to the skating rink, the mood was breezy.

TWO

A little while later, the Four Locos were chilling inside the skating rink where the action was in full swing. The place was packed with teenagers. As the rapper Key Glock's song "Bottom of the Pot" screamed through the speakers, girls from all over the city were popping and shaking so nasty that if Jesus Christ himself was in the building, he would've blushed.

Orlando whispered in some pretty little young girl's ear while Mason and Pancho were shooting dice with some Westside niggas in the restroom. Bruno was enjoying the scene, but his attention was focused on one girl in particular. Savannah. In Bruno's mind, Savannah was always the prettiest girl in the building. He had been crushing on her since second grade at Peter Crump Elementary School. She was a shy, skinny, hazel-eyed, yellow bone girl being raised by an aunt who didn't give a damn who she was with, where she was at, or what she was doing. Savannah's mother overdosed on cocaine back in the day and she had no idea who her father was. At the present time, she was twelve and involved in an unhealthy relationship with a dude named Alfonso Money who was eighteen. She meant nothing to him other than being used as a sex toy to set out for his homeboys whenever they felt the urge to fuck something. Bruno hated that she was being treated like this, but there was nothing he could do to stop it. Alfonso Money was a beast. So, as he stood there in the refreshment line, Bruno couldn't help walking over and flirting with her like he always did.

"What's up, Savannah, what's poppin'?"

"Nothin'. What's good wit you, Lil Bruno?" she popped back as her shiny, bubble gum flavored lip gloss made him feel some type of way.

"Just hanging out with my partners, ya feel me."

"Oh yea, The Four Locos, right?"

"You already know what time it is. Anyway, what ya drinkin'? Let me guess. A peach soda for Miss Savannah?"

"Naw, I hate peaches. I'm gettin' strawberry."

Bruno pulled two one-dollar bills from his pocket and handed it to the guy working the cash register.

"Two strawberry sodas, homie."

They grabbed their drinks and sat down at an open table. Those beautiful hazel eyes of hers seemed to burn holes straight through his soul as he struggled not to lose himself within them.

"Can I ask you somethin', Bruno?"

"Yeah," he answered quickly, beginning to lose himself already.

"Why you always so nice to me? I mean, I know you hear all that shit folks say about me. You could have any girl you want, but you over here wasting yo' time wit me."

Bruno's heart felt like it was going a hundred beats per second. But, before he could respond, his left jaw was slapped hard from the blind side. The entire left side of his face went numb and began swelling up to the size of a pumpkin. His arms and legs went offline, so getting back up on his feet appeared to be a mission impossible. The ceiling was spinning, and he was soaked in strawberry soda. A few seconds later, Alfonso sat on his chest, bitch slapping him over and over again. The slaps were so vicious that Bruno lost control and pissed himself. The slaps turned into punches and the punches escalated to his head being stomped out by a group of savage niggas. Orlando came charging in from out of nowhere, instantly putting three dudes to sleep with three wild haymakers. Mason and Poncho jumped in throwing punches with bad intentions, but it wasn't enough. The Four Locos were outnumbered by niggas who were stronger and older than they were. Suddenly two gunshots went off causing panic to rush through the crowd like Ron Artest. The party that started off as a young playa's paradise ended up being a death trap filled with teenagers, who were drunk with terror and running for their lives. As the crowd sprinted through the exit doors, Poncho and Mason lay beaten unconscious on the skating rink floor. Orlando, who'd been beaten badly himself, crawled over and held Bruno's head in his lap, who'd just been shot twice in the chest. Blood seemed to be leaking out of him from everywhere. His mouth couldn't form any words.

"Hold on, hood. Errthang gon' be aight, just keep breathing," Orlando pleaded, trying to motivate his best friend to stay alive.

"Somebody help him!" Savannah cried.

The last thing Bruno saw was the expression of fear written all over Orlando's face and then everything faded to black.

BRUNO WOKE up two days later inside of a recovery room at Jackson Hospital. IV fluid dripped and dropped from its transparent bag through sterilized tubing into his veins. An oxygen tube was placed inside of his nostrils so that his lungs were constantly drinking fresh air. If one of the bullets were a half inch further in either direction, he would've been dead. He was still a bit foggy but conscious as Madear and Bella hugged and loved on him like the last tall glass of cold ice water in the middle of an empty desert. They continued this sappy public display of affection until a night shift nurse finally forced them to go home and try to get some rest. Her last words of assurance to them were, *"He will be just fine in no time. He's in good hands with Jackson Hospital"*. It sounded good, but that night shift nurse had no idea about the dark thoughts swimming around inside of his head.

Finally alone, he slipped deep within himself inside of his cold dark hospital room. The silence was creepy, only interrupted by the constant noise made by the oxygen tank and hospital monitors he was hooked up to. Physically, Bruno Santana would recover. However, there was psychological damage that nobody was aware of. A certain blackness contaminated with rage flowed beneath the surface. The devil had tapped danced over his grave wearing two left boots. The old him had passed away and he lost himself. The second hand of the clock ticked. No more understanding. His path was cemented.

THREE

Several weeks later, Jackson Hospital released Bruno to his south side stomping grounds. His mother baked a chocolate upside down popcorn cake and invited his three best friends over to celebrate his homecoming. After everyone's stomach was full, the Four Locos sat outside on the front porch.

"For real though, bruh, errbody trippin' off that bullshit at the skating rink. But next time we run cross Alfonso, we gon' pain that fool, bruh. That's on errthang," Mason said while dapping up Bruno.

"On my mama," Poncho jumped in. "It's gon' be a Loco party off the intro. No questions asked. We gon' catch this clown and bust him in his shit. I swear to God, we gon' give that boy the bizness. We gon'-"

"Hold up, hood," Orlando interrupted before Poncho could finish talking shit. "That fool Alfonso ain't talkin' 'bout no fightin', bruh. That boy tried to kill you for nothing, Bruno. My cousin said we need to give that bitch nigga back what he gave us, and I'm down wit it."

Orlando pulled a .38 caliber Smith and Wesson snub nose undercover special from his pocket and handed it to Bruno.

"You 'bout that life, my nigga?"

Bruno held the cold steel in his hands and felt the tiny hairs on the back of his neck stand up. "Where you get that heat from?" he asked.

"My cousin Meatball from English Village gave it to me after that Looney's thing. He gave me four of 'em, so we all got one. Niggas gon' have to take us serious now. So, wassup, you 'bout it?"

"Yeah," Bruno said, looking Orlando straight in the eyes. "I'm with it."

They all knew it was time to grow up and be the predator rather than the prey. Fist fights were for kids who usually ended up with either the winner or the loser on the evening news with bullets buried inside their flesh. Nobody chooses to live by the gun, but in the streets, there is no time to whine and cry about how unfair the environment is. You either kill or be killed; that's just the way it is.

A couple hours later, after the homecoming party was over, Bruno sat on the front porch with Bella watching the sunset while trying to respond to her many questions.

"Why them boys hurt you, Bruno?"

"I guess 'cause they wanted to."

"Why?"

"I dunno, Bella. Maybe cause they ain't like me."

"Why they ain't like you?"

"I dunno."

"Well, I like you. You are the best big brudda in the whole wide world."

Bruno smiled and kissed her on the cheek. "I like you too, Bella, and you are the best little sister in the whole wide world."

Bella giggled as a white Monte Carlo pulled up in front of the house. The guy driving the car was a man called Big. Big was in his late 50's. He was a street hustler who had a mean reputation of getting money by any means necessary. He rolled down his window on the driver side and signaled Bruno to come over.

"Go on in the house, Bella, and find something to watch on tv. I'll be inside in a minute."

"Ok." She hopped up and skipped inside of the house.

Bruno walked over to the Monte Carlo, curious as to what Big wanted.

"Wassup, Big?"

"What up, lil Bruno. I heard you bumped heads with that bitch ass nigga Alfonso. You aight?"

"Yeah. He shot me 'cause he caught me talkin' to Savannah."

"Well, I ain't surprised 'bout that. These dudes animals out here, lil homie. You learned that shit the hard way, but at least you learned it. In the end, that's all that matters. Life ain't nuthin' but a crap game. You gon' always lose more times than you win. The goal is to win as much as you can before you crap out. And don't get it twisted, eventually you will crap out. We all will. That's the law of nature. You ain't 'posed to spare none of these niggas out here, lil homie, 'cause you can bet yo' life ain't none of 'em gon' spare you. You got a strap?"

"Yeah, I got a lil somethin'," he said, lifting his shirt to show the gun sitting on his waist.

"True that. And if you draw down, you better use it. And if you smoke somebody, you smoke everybody wit 'em. Don't leave no witnesses, you understand?"

"Yea, I understand."

"That's good, homie. Ya see, this ain't advice on how to be a productive citizen. This is advice on how to stay alive. Now go out there and rep ya hood. It's yo' time now. Make 'em respect and fear ya. And if you ever need me for anything, just holla at me."

"I'ma do that, bruh. I 'preciate it."

As Big drove off down the street, his words danced around inside of Bruno's head like Sammy Davis Jr. on a hardwood floor in hell. *"It's yo' time now. Make 'em respect and fear ya."*

Those words he would never ever forget.

FOUR

P am Parker was a forty-year-old white female with
extremely low self-esteem and very little money. She was
living hand to mouth in a tiny two-bedroom trailer inside of the
Montgomery Regency trailer park off Troy Highway. She felt
trapped by the hand that life dealt her. She was stuck with a
dead-end gig, and the responsibility to raise a child she didn't
give birth to. Her worthless, drug addict sister Sharon had
gotten herself knocked up by some random low-class black
dude who couldn't support himself, much less a baby. Sharon
had abused one too many drugs in her day. Too many rules and
not enough booze was her motto back then.

One fall evening at the Doby's Inn, a pay by the hour motel
on the Mobile Highway, Sharon hooked up with a dusty ass
junky she'd met at the Top Flight Night Club across the street
from Two Lane Court. They were both drinking like out-of-
control Irish Sailors. But Sharon, who'd been banging good
cocaine all day, had gotten too high. She got so high she never
came back down. She was buried in a small rundown cemetery
located off Ann Street. Savannah was four-years-old when she

died and Pam became the legal guardian over a motherless child. She resented having Savannah around and made it obviously clear in all her dealings with the young girl. On this particular occasion, during the wee hours of the morning, Pam was hugged up on a raggedy black pleather sofa inside the living room. She was flirting with her brand-new promising possibility for a companion, Hank. The drunken truck driver from Covington County. He was her top priority for the time being.

"No more of this lovey dovey crap until you get us some more alcohol," Hank slurred.

"You already drank everything I got in the house. It's over with. Now it's time for us to spend some quality time together!" Pam shot back.

"Quality time? You can't be serious! Look in the mirror, Peggy, Pam, or whatever the hell your name is! You 'bout as smart as a pile of horse shit and yo' conversation 'bout as interesting as a bowl of hot piss! If you don't get some alcohol in here, like right now, this lil spend the night wit a whore shit is over!"

The entire atmosphere changed inside the trailer, including Pam's attitude.

"Hold on, Hank, I'm sorry. I never should've got you worked up like this," Pam pleaded as if her life was on the line. "It's my fault. I'll get you some more alcohol. Savannah! Savannah! Get your ass in here right now!" Pam yelled, waking the poor child from her peaceful slumber.

Savannah jumped out of bed, threw on a pair of sweatpants, an Alabama State University hooded sweatshirt, and her low-top Reebok sneakers. She stumbled into the living room to see what her wicked aunt wanted.

"What did I do now, Pam?" Savannah asked, fully dressed but sleepy-eyed.

"What haven't you done, Savannah? That's a stupid question. Anyway, I need you to grab me and Hank about twenty dollars' worth of beer from the store. I'm sure something is open," she informed Savannah while handing her two crumpled up ten-dollar bills.

"But it's late, Pam, and I gotta go to school in the morning."

"What you have to do is what I tell you to do, so don't make me repeat myself again."

"But where am I supposed to get it from?"

"That's not my problem. Now go, dammit!" Pam snapped.

Savannah snatched the money from Pam's hand and stormed out the front door of the trailer. It was 3:34am.

FIVE

Orlando laid stretched out on the couch wearing a pair of red basketball shorts and a white tank top while watching television. He puffed deeply on a wine flavored Swisher stuffed with fluffy Sour Diesel buds. He was high as a kite and enjoying every second of it. Just as he was about to blow out another cloud into the environment, his mother unlocked the front door, stumbled inside the house, and plopped beside him on the couch. She smelled like the inside of a Hennessy bottle. At the age of thirty, she was still young, and her youthful attractiveness hadn't betrayed her yet. Her name was Kandi Beard, but everyone called her Candy. Candy had hooked up with Orlando's father Antonio during her senior year in high school. Antonio was a twenty-nine-year-old low-level hustler from the Vineyard. He was in no danger of being accused as the brightest bulb in the box, but what he lacked in intelligence, he made up for with pretty words and heavy hands. Candy was barely eighteen when their paths crossed. She was a young, dumb, gorgeous, dark-skinned dime with a body like Buffy and the IQ of a teenage Jessica Simpson.

Antonio was dressed so sharp the day they were introduced to each other you could've sliced homemade bread with his swag. No question about it, Candy was hooked. In a matter of weeks, she believed Antonio was God's gift to all women. Whatever he said or did, she took to heart. And whatever he asked of her, she did without question. She was sprung. A few months after receiving the title of Antonio's girl, Candy ended up pregnant with Orlando.

So, with a bun in the oven and her knight in pimped out shining armor standing by her side, Candy's picture-perfect plan for living happily ever after was within arm's reach. However, all her hopes and dreams came tumbling down like Jack and Jill the night Antonio beat a sixteen-year-old prostitute to death for holding back some money she owed him outside of a Greyhound bus station on West Boulevard. He was sentenced to life in prison without the possibility of parole in the Alabama Department of Corrections. Candy was left alone to raise an inmate's bastard baby all by herself. The situation was filthy, and the future seemed grim except Antonio had taught Candy how to survive through hard times. *"When in doubt, set it out,"* he used to always tell her. So, when the monthly bills were due or it was time to put food on the table, she sold her body to a long line of older men who were willing to cover the high price tag for the ultimate girlfriend experience. Candy worked as a high-class escort throughout Orlando's childhood. Therefore, when she sat down beside him on the couch that night drunk and banged out, it was nothing out of the ordinary in Orlando's eyes.

"What up, Mama, long night?"

"Hell yeah. I spent the last few hours with these three old men-"

"That's ight, I don't wanna know," Orlando interrupted.

"My bad, baby, I just had a lil too much to drink."

"You ate somethin'?" he asked.

"Nah, but I'm alright. Just let me hit some of that green you too young to be smoking on."

"You need to put some food in ya stomach, Mama," he said as he passed the blunt.

Candy took three deep pulls of the blunt, inhaling its mystical marijuana smoke, and blew it out as she rested her head gently on Orlando's shoulder.

"Are you worried about your mama, baby?"

"I just want you to be ok."

"I promise, I'll be ok."

"Aight, Mama."

"How lil Bruno doin'?" she asked.

"He doin' aight."

"That's good. Tell him I asked 'bout him."

"Alright, Mama."

Candy took four more puffs on the blunt. "You plan on going to school in the morning?" she asked.

"Yeah, I think so," Orlando said, a little too high.

"Good. Well, you need to get some sleep. It'll be time to get up soon."

"Ok," he said as Candy handed the blunt back to him.

She pulled herself up from the couch and made her way towards the bedroom. "And, Orlando, don't ever forget, I love you, baby boy," she called from the hallway.

"I love you too, Mama."

Orlando put the blunt out in the ashtray, turned the television down and drifted off into LaLa land. It was 3:34am.

SIX

As Poncho slept peacefully on his worn twin size mattress inside his typical teenage bedroom that looked as if it'd been hit by a tornado, he was awakened by a tapping sound coming from the window. He sat up, stretched and wiped the leftover crusty sleep from his tired eyes. It took a minute for his brain to crank up, but once it was in full throttle, he rolled out of bed and opened the window. Just as he expected, Mason was standing there in the middle of the night with a smile as wide as a prostitute's snatch. He was dressed in all black and carrying a black backpack.

"You just gon' stand there like a clown or you comin' in?" Poncho joked.

Mason quickly but silently climbed in through the window, careful not to wake Poncho's parents who were asleep inside their bedroom. It's not because his parents would be angry that Mason was there, he was basically a member of the family. They were hard working people who needed every minute of sleep they could get to maintain their busy lives. From six in the morning until two in the evening, Monday through Friday, Poncho's dad worked at the Rheems Manufacturing Plant. After that, from three in the evening until midnight, he worked as a security guard at the lumber yard on Air Base Boulevard. On the weekends, from sunup until sundown, he cut grass and did odd jobs wherever he could find the work. His wife Carmen worked just as hard as he did. She was a full-time maid for a wealthy retired couple who lived in the Old Cloverdale neighborhood. On the weekends, she sold candy, pastries and cold sodas to the kids in the Regency Park neighborhood. She did all of that and still found time to raise her only child Poncho. His parents were the definition of hard work and determination. After they illegally crossed the border from Mexico in the United States two years before Poncho was born, they appreciated the chance to work harder for less money than the true-blue Americans were making. They weren't in search of overnight success. They believed that a race isn't won by the swift, but by those who endured to the end. And that's exactly what they did, building a decent life for themselves in Montgomery, Alabama. A life they had every right to be proud of.

Now Mason, on the other hand, was from a completely different bloodline. His dad was a mentally retarded man who fell in love at first sight with a morbidly obese young girl in a movie theater and brutally raped her in the parking lot. In those days, black folks weren't having abortions, so his mom was forced to raise a baby she hated. Every time she looked him in the eyes, she was reminded of that night. She often fantasized about putting a pillow over his face and suffocating him. She knew without a shadow of a doubt that he would grow up to be a slimy piece of shit just like his father. For the first few years of his life, he prayed intensely that he would die in his sleep or get snatched from his crib, never to be seen or heard from again. As Mason got older, her hate for this child only intensified. When he was five years old, she mixed a razor blade in his food, hoping to kill the curse she'd given birth to. Lucky for Mason, the razor got stuck in the roof of his mouth. He ended up in the hospital requiring stitches while she ended up having to answer a lot of questions from a CPS worker. Needless to say, from that day on, she settled with beating his black ass every day instead of risking a possible prison sentence.

But that's neither here nor there. As of right now, Mason and Poncho were working on a plan they'd put together a week ago to stack some paper. Poncho knew an older white man from the Eastside who'd pay fifty bucks a piece for as many brand name car radios as he could get. So, he recruited his best friend Mason to be his partner in this business venture. Their goal was to stack a thousand bucks, use the cash to buy a pound of marijuana, become the biggest dope boys in Regency Park, and live their lives like ballers.

"How many you get?"

"I got five of 'em. Two Clarions, two Pioneers, and a Kenwood. How many is that all together?"

"Twelve," Poncho replied with a grin on his face. "We almost there."

"We need eight more. I can get 'em like right now," Mason said.

"Nah, hood. It's late. We can get the rest of 'em tomorrow night."

"Bet. If that's how you wanna play it."

"Yeah. You goin' hard, hood. But go too hard and you gon' end up in the county jail. Besides, we gotta go to school in the morning."

"You right, bruh," Mason agreed.

"You stayin' here tonight or what?"

"Might as well," Mason said as he snatched the blanket off Poncho's bed and laid down on the floor.

After a few moments of silence passed... "Oh, Poncho?"

"Wassup, hood?"

"I love you, bruh. Goodnight."

"Shut the hell up, hood."

Mason laughed. It was 3:34am.

SEVEN

Aremote jungle located halfway between the middle of nowhere and no return. It was Cicely Tyson dark there because the sun doesn't shine in that part of the world. What part of the world was it? Well, your guess is as good as any because location, location, location was the last thing on his mind at this point. His only objective was to get gone as fast and as far away as possible. He was being stalked by wild savages he couldn't describe. Even though he'd never communicated with any of them, he believed their intentions were to capture, butcher and serve his mutilated body around the table for a down home savage family dinner. He could smell their savage, mouthwatering, wild dog saliva while the sound of obnoxious growling stomachs assaulted his eardrums like Ray Rice on a drunk girl's face. He could feel them quickly closing in on him. Just as his heart was about to leap out of his chest from fear, he sat up in his bed soaked in a cold sweat, alone in his dark bedroom. Bruno fought to catch his breath as the branded gunshot wounds on his chest felt like they were burning him alive. He dryly swallowed three of the horse sized pills his doctor had prescribed for pain. Bruno dreaded the nightmares he'd experienced since arriving home from the hospital. However, there was really nothing he could do about them. Drowsy from the medication but too shook up to go back to LaLa land, Bruno decided to go for a ride in hopes of relaxing his badly rattled nerves. He threw on his Auburn University jacket and crept out of the crib. It was 3:34am. The morning air was Frosty the Snowman cold with a wind so strong it felt as if the city of Montgomery was a giant birthday cake and Jack Frost was attempting to blow out its candles. Bruno zipped up the jacket, jumped on his Mongoose bike and took off on a morning ride. The fresh air worked magic by making his migraine magically disappear. While pedaling down Troy Highway, he recognized a familiar face walking inside of the Petro gas station. There she was, a sight for sore eyes, Savannah Parker.

His first instinct was to just keep on pedaling because more than likely she was with her boyfriend Alfonso. Then he thought to himself, screw it. He pulled his bike up to the store front and waited for her to come out. It didn't take long, but once she exited the store and realized Bruno was standing there, she froze as if she was in the presence of a ghost.

"Wassup, Savannah."

"Hey, Bruno," she said nervously.

"I saw you walking in the store and thought I'd stop and speak."

"Are you mad at me?" she asked.

"Nah. I ain't got nothin' to be mad at you 'bout."

She caught Bruno off guard by hugging him so tight he thought his ribcage was going to crack.

"I was so scared. I thought you were dead," she said, her eyes misty with wet tears.

"Nah, I ain't dead."

"No duh. If you were, we wouldn't be talking right now," she said sarcastically while wiping a few tears from her face.

"Yeah. I guess you right about that."

"I'm just playing," she said.

"So, what you doin' out so late?"

"Well, let's see. My stupid aunt and her dumb friend wanted some beer and thought I should be the one to go get it. Then I walked all the way down here and the guy in there tells me I can't buy none with no ID."

"That sucks."

"Yeah, tell me 'bout it."

A nervous silence filled the air.

"I was thinking maybe we could go chill or somethin'?" Bruno asked in a shaky voice.

"Sounds good, but I gotta find somewhere to get some beer or my aunt gon' go all super bitch on me. Maybe some other time."

He couldn't believe his ears. What were the odds? Some quality one on one time with Savannah. A little carefree chit chat. A casual conversation with his pretty-eyed dream girl on a dreary Monday morning in March. *Chill out, Bruno,* he told himself. *Don't start acting like a lame.* He had to regain his composure if he planned on impressing her in any kind of meaningful way.

"I might be able to get that beer for your aunt," he said.

"How? You must know the guy working in the store or something?"

"Naw, but I gotta plan that might work."

"What kind of plan?" she asked, doubt written all over her face.

"Come on. I'll show you."

They walked inside the gas station holding hands like two high school sweethearts. Bruno grabbed two cases of Budweiser from the cooler, walked up to the cashier and dropped the beer on the counter. The cashier was a skinny middle-aged Arab guy who was visibly annoyed by these two underaged drinkers trying to cop some alcohol.

"Look! I told your lil girlfriend here the same thing I'm telling you. No I.D., no beer!"

Bruno reached under his jacket, pulled out his gun and pointed it at the Arab's face. "This the only I.D. I got."

The sight of the chrome pistol in his face drained the Arab of all his courage. "Please don't kill me. I have kids. Just take the beer and money. I no tell the police. I swear."

"I know you won't 'cause if you do, I'll come back and kill you. Understand?"

"Yes, I understand. Please, just take it and go," he said, handing him the beer and money.

Bruno walked backwards out of the store while dragging a stunned Savannah by her hand. He told her to sit on the handlebars and hold the beer. She complied. After they arrived at Savannah's trailer, she hurried inside to give her aunt the beer. When she came back out, Bruno was sitting on the Mongoose bike smiling at her.

"Oh my God! You're freaking crazy!" she shouted.

"Nah. I ain't crazy. You needed somethin' and I got it for you."

"Where'd you get a gun from?"

"I just got one, ya feel me."

"Nah, I don't feel ya. You gon' end up in jail doin' dumb stuff like that."

"Yea, yea, yea. But, are you and me straight?"

Attempting to hold it back, she couldn't stop herself from allowing a small smile to grace her pretty face.

"Yeah, we straight, Bruno," she said.

He was as happy as a coke head at an all-you-can-snort cocaine buffet. Now was the time.

"Hey, you wanna go do somethin'?" he asked.

"Do what?" she asked surprisingly.

"It's a surprise."

"It ain't got nothin' to do with guns, do it?"

"Nah, I think you'll like it."

"Okay. Let's go."

She sat on the bike's handlebars as Bruno pedaled out of the trailer park headed down the Troy Highway. His precious Savannah was smiling the whole way.

EIGHT

Exactly twenty-two minutes and thirty-four seconds later, Bruno and Savannah lounged across from each other in a booth at the Waffle House on Troy Highway. They had already placed their orders for waffles, scrambled eggs, grits, bacon, sausage patties, orange juice and a couple slices of pecan pie. There was no way they were going to down all of that, but Bruno was throwing no dice in an attempt to impress Miss Savannah. He even ordered a cup of Joe to show her how much of a grown man he really was.

When the middle-aged, big-breasted woman asked how he wanted his coffee, he looked at her like she was trippin and said, "I want it hot. How do you think I want it?"

The waitress was tickled by this little puppy pretending to be a big dog and brought him exactly what he asked for. Hot, black coffee, no sugar or cream. He took a swig of the hot, bitter liquid and if it wasn't for Savannah sitting across from him, he would've spit it back inside the mug. It was the nastiest crap he'd ever tasted in his life. He couldn't understand how grown folks drank so much of that shit. But he didn't dare let

Savannah know how he felt because that would've blown his manly image. Instead, he set the mug down and never picked it back up again. After the food arrived, they played around, joked, made funny faces at one another and fed each other like a newlywed couple on a Hawaiian honeymoon. They were having the time of their young lives.

"It's 'cause I like you," Bruno said out of nowhere.

"What?" Savannah asked, confused.

"That night at Looney's you asked me why I treated you so nice. It's 'cause I like you."

"Oh," Savannah said as she stared down at her plate hoping Bruno didn't notice how hard she was blushing.

"My bad. I ain't mean to upset you."

"You ain't upset me. I just didn't know you liked me like that."

"Well, now you know."

"Yeah, now I know."

There was another moment of awkward silence.

"Can I ask you something, Bruno?"

"Yeah."

"Why the police ain't lock Alfonso up for shooting you?"

"'Cause they ain't know he shot me."

"Why you ain't tell on him? It would've made everything easier."

"'Cause I ain't no snitch."

"Oh," she said as she popped a piece of pecan pie in her mouth.

Breakfast with Savannah was sweeter than homemade biscuits smothered in Alaga syrup. After they left the diner, headed back up Troy Highway, they rode in perfect silence. Meaningless constant conversation wasn't necessary. They were completely in tune with each other like a happy couple who'd been together for years. The mood was slow rolling and the road that led back to Savannah's neighborhood was lit up by their smiles. It was 5:45am when they pulled up in front of the trailer. She hopped down off the bike's handlebars and turned around to face Bruno who'd already laid the bike on its side.

"I had fun, Bruno. I hope we can do this again sometime."

"Yeah, me too," he said, handing her his phone number, not sure what to do next.

Suddenly, she wrapped her arm around his neck and kissed him like he'd never been kissed before. Their tongues dirty danced in each other's mouth to the sound of their pounding hearts. Once they finally separated, their eyes remained intensely focused on each other.

"So, do we go together now?" he asked in a dark, determined voice.

"What about Alfonso?" she responded, trying to catch her breath.

"Fuck, Alfonso," he said.

"Yeah, fuck him," she agreed.

They were now officially in a relationship. Again, he kissed his girlfriend.

NINE

It was 7:00am as Orlando made his way on foot through the early morning rain to catch the school bus headed to Floyd Jr. High School. He was still baked from all the dope he'd blown earlier that morning. So high, in fact, that he almost talked himself into saying the hell with it and skipping school altogether. Somehow, he found the energy to get up, eat a candy bar and make his way to the bus stop for school. When he got there, Poncho and a few other kids were standing in the rain patiently waiting for the school bus.

"Wassup, hood. Where Mason and Bruno at?" Orlando asked.

"You already know Mason ain't comin', he never do. And Bruno ain't coming either. I stopped by his crib this mornin' and he was on some roses are red, violets are blue shit wit Savannah on the phone. I guess they call themselves goin' together now or whatever," Poncho said.

"Savannah and Bruno? I can't believe that fool finally got the courage up to ask that chick out. That boy been sweatin' her for a long ass time."

"I know right, but that fool done more than asked her out. They went out to eat 'bout three or four this morning and guess how he paid for it."

"How he paid?" Orlando asked curiously.

"He robbed the Petro this morning."

"Hell naw," Orlando whispered in shock.

"Yeah the fuck he did, and Savannah was right there with him. That boy hit for five hundred dollars. I seen the bread myself. That nigga ain't bullshittin'. Then him and Savannah went to the Waffle House and balled out."

"Damn. That fool done stepped it all the way up. My loco Bruno," Orlando said excitedly.

"Hell yeah. Bruno 'bout that life. Now everybody gon' have to step up. Ya feel me, loco?"

"Fasho. We gon' holla at them fools when school get out. That boy trippin'," Orlando said, laughing.

The long, dirty, yellow school bus pulled up to the bus stop and opened its doors so the neighborhood kids could file inside. Orlando was amped from the news about Bruno.

"Loco Gang, hood!" Orlando yelled out the window as the bus pulled off.

"Shut yo' dumb ass up!" some hood chick snapped from somewhere inside the bus.

TEN

It was half past noon. Icy cold water leaked from the heavens inside of chubby, slow falling raindrops. The sky was a dull shade of gray as thunder boomed in the background, aggressively interrupting Mother Nature's teary-eyed tantrum. Bruno lounged on the front porch of his crib, deep in thought, blowing his last blunt of Reggie Miller into outer space. During a moment of multiple thoughts running wildly inside his head, Mason rode up on the front lawn. He laid his Mongoose bike down on its side and sprinted for the porch to get out of the rain.

"Wassup, Bruno? If I knew you weren't at school, I woulda been came through," Mason said.

"Nah, hood, I wasn't feeling it today. What you got goin' on?" Bruno asked as he dapped him up.

"Same ole. Same ole. Just tryna find me a come up. Ya feel me?"

"True that. I got a lil sumthin' I been puttin' together inside my head," Bruno said, passing Mason the blunt.

"Oh yeah? Then go on lace me up. I'm down for the come up."

"Bet that up. I been sittin' here thinkin' 'bout things all morning. I done seen fools riding by in dope ass whips on shiny wheels wit car hoppers kissin' and lovin' on 'em. Clowns livin' life like Kings wit they flashy chains and high-priced clothes tellin' do boy niggas how it is and how things gon' go, ya feel me? Then I seen maggot niggas walkin' 'round dressed like bumpkins and asking other maggots fa spare change and loose cigarettes. But I'm like fuck all that. I ain't tryna be like these nobody ass clowns. I want us to be on top, ya feel me. But talkin' 'bout it ain't gon' get us nothin'. We gotta be 'bout it, ya feel me? We gotta step up."

"So, what you wanna do?" Mason asked with a twisted smile on his face.

"I want what them baller boys got and I wanna take it from 'em."

"So, what you talkin' 'bout, robbin' these fools or sumthin'?"

"Yeah. I know a dude who stash all his work at his grandma's house over in King Hill. She works at night on the weekends from ten to six in the morning. The house be empty. The dude stashed the work in a old deep freezer in the basement. It's a easy lick. We just gotta hit it."

"I'm feelin' it. That shit sound sweet," Mason said, smiling.

"It is sweet."

"Who put you on the lick?" Mason asked.

"My girl put me on it this mornin'."

"Yo' girl? Who yo' girl?" Mason asked, feeling lost.

"Savannah Parker."

"You and Savannah together?" Mason asked, laughing.

Bruno shot up to his feet and stared Mason in the eye. "Yeah, she mine now. You gotta problem wit it?"

"Hell nah, hood. You know it ain't like that. I'm happy fa y'all," Mason said. "You talkin' 'bout robbin' Alfonso, ain't it?"

"Yeah. That's who it is. And if y'all ain't down, I'll do it by myself, ya feel me?"

"Come on, Bruno. You know I'm down and when Poncho and Orlando hear 'bout it, they gon' be down too."

"That's wassup. So, we doin' this?"

"I'm wit you, hood. Fuck Alfonso."

"Yeah, fuck that clown."

A silence crept between them as the raindrops continued to fall. Mason broke the silence.

"Don't get mad at me, Bruno, but do Savannah know she yo' girlfriend? If she don't then she really ain't yours. That just make you a stalker."

Bruno laughed as the rain kept pouring down.

ELEVEN

Savannah lounged on the bed inside her small bedroom beside her best and only friend in the city, Mia Monroe. The two preteens had been inseparable since knee-high. They would burn hours upon hours talking about fashion, jealous hoodrats, and their favorite subject of all, boys. Mia was a cute, skinny, mocha skinned shawty who, at only twelve, considered herself an expert on any and everything concerning the male gender. She knew their thoughts, motivations, and what outfits to rock that would have any guy eating out the palm of her hand. There was no doubt in anyone's mind why she and Savannah were homegirls. Currently, they were applying each other's manicures while jamming to Hot 105.7 on the boombox and participating in their favorite pastime. Gossiping.

"Gurl, when Tammy walked in class this morning wearing that purple bubble suit with that pink bow on the back, I thought I was gon' die tryin' not to crack up!" Mia said, laughing. "She looked like a giant Christmas present."

"Oh my God. What was she thinking?" Savannah asked.

"She was thinking she looked good, that's what."

"If I was there, I probably would've laughed in her face."

"I know you would've, and I would've laughed too 'cause you was laughing."

"Yup, 'cause you crazy like that, gurl."

"Speaking of... Why you ain't come to school? Let me guess, you done got back with Alfonso?"

"Naw, gurl, Alfonso old news. I got a new man now," Savannah revealed, blushing.

"What? Who yo' man? What he look like?" Mia asked with a fake look of disbelief on her face.

"Don't worry 'bout all that. Just know me and my man'll be aight."

"Oh, so you got secrets now. Well, just don't let Alfonso find out. You see what he did to Lil Bruno at the skating rink," Mia said, blowing on her nails that were still wet with pink cotton candy fingernail polish.

"Bruno ain't worried 'bout Alfonso or nobody else. He done changed, gurl."

Mia eyed Savannah suspiciously. "Let me find out Lil Bruno yo' secret friend."

"So what if he is?" Savannah asked defensively.

"Nothin'. Lil Bruno kinda cute in a lil kid type of way."

"Yeah, and he really cool too. He ain't stuck up or nothing."

"Gurl, you know you ain't gotta sell him to me. If you like him, I like him."

Savannah smiled, unable to stop herself from blushing. "Yeah, I like him."

"I can tell. You know I gotta get you, gurl," Mia started singing. "Savannah and Bruno sittin' in a tree, k-i-s-s-i-n-g. First comes love, then comes marriage. Then came the baby in a baby carriage."

Both chicks started giggling.

TWELVE

Around six o'clock that evening at Trenholm Court Projects, the rain had finally ceased. That worked out well for Mary Evans because now she could fire up the grill to prepare her oldest son's favorite meal: grilled polish sausage and deer burgers. His name was Alberto Money. He was twenty-four and currently serving in the United States military, stationed at Tinker Air Force Base in Oklahoma City, Oklahoma. Mary was obviously proud of him. He had his head on straight and loved her deeply. When she found out he took a week off from serving his country so he could travel home for a visit, she was in hog heaven. She prayed he could talk his younger brothers, Alfonso, eighteen and Abraham, sixteen, into getting their lives on track. All of them were together under the same roof, so she stepped outside to work magic on the grill while the three men she cherished most talked amongst themselves.

"Listen, Alberto..."

"No, Alfonso. I don't want to hear it. I just want you to answer my question with a simple yes or no answer. Did you or did you not shoot some thirteen-year-old kid over a twelve-year-old girl you was sleeping with?" Alberto demanded.

"Yeah, I did, but I was drunk and faded, Big. I flipped out."

"Stupid nigga! Don't you know you too old to be screwing with a twelve-year-old girl? That's statutory rape. You act like you tryna go to prison."

"Naw, he ain't tryna go to the joint. He just lame as hell," Abraham said, laughing.

"Abraham, go outside and help Ma with the food. You and I will talk later," Alberto said.

"Come on, I wanna hear this."

"Don't make me tell you twice, boy."

"Aight, aight, I'm outta here."

Abraham checked to make sure his heat was secure on his waist and walked out the front door.

"Look, Alfonso. I love ya and I ain't tryna to beat you up, but you gotta get yo' eyes focused on the big picture. I got folks calling me all the way in Oklahoma 'bout you shootin' that kid and messin' 'round wit that lil girl. You know you wrong for that. You makin' our whole family look like a freak show. The world is a lot bigger than Trenholm Court and Montgomery, Alabama. You can have it all and be whatever you wanna be, but you can't be nothing from behind some prison wall or from a casket. You a senior in high school now. You gotta start thinkin' 'bout yo' future and yo' family. Abraham looks up to you and wanna be just like you. And mama stressing, worried 'bout you day and night. You gotta grow up and do the right thing, bruh. Me, you, Abraham, mama and grandma is family. We all we got. We gotta make it, bruh."

"You right. I promise I'ma try and get it together, big bruh," Alfonso said.

"That's all I'm asking from ya, bruh. Just try. I mean really try."

"I was thinkin' 'bout joining the military after graduation. You know, aim high, be all I can be and all that other shit."

"Like I said, you can be and do whatever you put yo' mind to, lil bruh," Alberto said, laughing.

"Oh yeah, I meant to tell you earlier. You can get my bed. I'll sleep on the couch while you in town," Alfonso offered.

"I 'preciate it, lil bruh, but I'm staying at grandma's house while I'm down here. Spend some time with her and check out some of these thick sistahs in King Hill I miss so much. See what they talkin' 'bout. I ain't been out there in a minute."

"Yeah. They out there and still crazy but fine as frog hair," Alfonso said.

"That's what I wanted to hear. Let's go see wassup wit mama, Abraham and this food. I'm starvin'."

The two young men walked out the door. The mood was chill, and the love was brotherly.

THIRTEEN

The aroma flowing from the kitchen had Bruno's stomach growling like an old pickup truck motor. Fried pork chops, mashed potatoes with brown gravy, biscuits, green string Brunos and strawberry ice cream for dessert. Savannah was showing off in the kitchen for her boyfriend. Not only was she a cutie, but she also inherited the cooking skills of a seventy-year-old, overweight, black as night grandmama from the sticks on her father's side. Bruno slouched on her couch watching the Atlanta Hawks play against the Chicago Bulls while trying to forget how hungry he was. Even Savannah's Aunt Pam didn't mind Bruno being treated like a king inside her home. After all, he did show up at her door with a hundred and fifty bucks worth of groceries and two cases of Budweiser from Mr. Meats grocery store as an icebreaker. She actually told him he was welcome in her home any time then bounced into her bedroom and got private with the two cases of beer and a plate. Savannah had never seen her aunt treat anyone with such hospitality. Instead of trying to figure it out, she just enjoyed the moment. The meal was delicious. Bruno had chewed so much of it he thought his gut would bust. Savannah thought to herself that Bruno was nothing like Alfonso. Bruno made a big deal over every little thing she did for him and showed appreciation for her doing it. He made her feel special which was a feeling she'd never experienced in her life. She felt like she could be herself around him without being criticized or judged. She felt that no matter what the scenario was, as long as she belonged to him, everything was going to be alright. So, as the two of them cuddled on the couch watching the basketball game, she knew she was truly in love with him.

"You want some more strawberry ice cream?" Savannah asked.

"Nah, I can't eat nothing else."

"Then how 'bout some coffee?" she said jokingly. They both started laughing.

"Are you making fun of me?" he asked.

"Yup," she said, kissing him on the cheek.

"Well, you better be careful 'cause I beat up folks who make fun of me."

"Everybody except for me," she said, kissing him again.

"Can I ask you somethin'?" he asked.

"Yup."

"Since I'm your boyfriend, do you have to do what I tell you to do?"

"Only if you have to do what I tell you to do, too."

"Okay. So, what you want me to do?" he asked.

"I want you to forget Alfonso and get paid some other way."

"Aight then, you ain't gotta do what I say," he conceded.

"That's messed up, Bruno."

"Ain't it though?" he said, smooching her on the lips.

FOURTEEN

Friday rolled around like the little white ball on a roulette table in Vegas. The Locos showed up locked and loaded. Orlando had convinced his second cousin WhichAway into driving them to King Hill to hit the lick. WhichAway was a sixteen-year-old loudmouth kid who considered himself a major player. However, those who were raised around him knew he was a major screw up. All he had to do was provide the ride, so how much trouble could he cause? Right before they split from Regency Park, Bruno amped The Locos up with a few last words.

"The world is made of two kinds of people," he said. "Cowards and gangsters. Tonight we gon' show the gangsta Gods what type of gangstas we is. See y'all in hell, Locos."

The lick instantly went from being about a payday to something much more. Destiny. There were no words left to be spoken. The young Locos cruised from Regency Park to King Hill in absolute silence. They were all distant in their thoughts. If they failed, they'd just be more knucklehead youngsters who should've never jumped off the porch. In the other corner, if they succeeded, they would be Gods. Eternal life was on the line. There was no turning back now.

The directions to the house Savannah gave Bruno were on point. It was game time.

"Cut off the lights and park at the corner," Bruno ordered as they drove past the targeted house.

It was 2:00am. The street was as empty as a meth addict's mouth. No one was watching out of the windows or wandering through the shadows. Inside the car, hearts raced beside sweaty palms. WhichAway nervously parked the car.

"Y'all ready?"

"Yeah, we ready, Bruno," Orlando answered for everybody.

"Alright, let's go get it."

They exited the car. Orlando, Poncho and Mason followed directly behind Bruno. Cool as cucumbers, they marched towards the lick about three houses down from where the Regal was parked. Once their Nike shoes touched the target's lawn, they sprinted to the backyard. A sliding glass door revealed darkness inside the house. There was no sign of the homeowner's presence anywhere. So far, so good.

"I got da hammer. You want me to buss da glass?" Poncho whispered.

Bruno tried the door and to everyone's surprise, it slid open. He thought to himself, *We really are being blessed by the Gangster Gods.*

The Locos crept inside the house. The interior was illuminated by an outside streetlight. The house was immaculately clean. There was a brown leather sectional sofa, a mahogany coffee table, and a large floor model television in the living room. Pictures of smiling faces, young and old, were displayed in frames on the walls. When they walked into the kitchen, they saw hotdogs and burgers sitting inside an aluminum pan on the kitchen table. Mason told himself, *I gotta grab that spread on the way out.* He was so hungry he could've literally eaten a Westside whore. Next to the icebox was a door that led to the basement, exactly where Savannah said it would be. Bruno opened it and made his way down the stairs with his Locos trailing. There was a light switch on a wall at the bottom of the stairs. Bruno flipped it on and the room was dustier than a Nigerian's foot. A stale smell hung in the air. Cobwebs, brown boxes and old furniture cluttered the spot, but no one gave it a second thought because sitting nonchalantly in the basement's rear was the lick.

FIFTEEN

The Locos stood around Bruno in anticipation as he opened the deep freezer's door. All their hopes and dreams were wrapped up in this lick like Christmas gifts underneath the Christmas trees. Poncho's left eye was twitching. Orlando's palms were itching. The tiny hairs on Mason's neck stood at full attention. Emotionally, they were riding a roller coaster ride. The coaster went up then came down. The freezer was filled with bags of trash, old clothes, Ebony magazines from the 80s, broken toys, and twisted up Christmas decorations. A whole lot of nothing.

"Man, ain't nothing there. That bitch done sent us on a pookie," Orlando complained.

"I knew it was too good to be true. All for nothing," Poncho whispered.

They bitched and moaned. Meanwhile, Bruno continued digging through the pile of debris. That's when he saw it. A swollen Nike gym bag buried beneath the trash. He pulled it out then laid it on the ground. Everyone was silent as he unzipped the bag. Inside was a blessing from the gangster God. Eight large ziplock bags stuffed with lime green marijuana and two bags filled with snow white cocaine. The last bag held multiple fat knots of hundred-dollar bills wrapped in rubber bands. The coaster went up.

"We rich, hood! We rich!" Mason shouted while jumping around as if he'd won the lottery. Poncho and Orlando hugged each other. They were on cloud nine. Their dreams had come true. They wanted to celebrate.

"Y'all niggas chill," Bruno said. "We gotta get out of here. Poncho, go get WhichAway and tell him to pull the car up in front of the house to pick us up."

"Aight, Bruno."

Poncho took off up the stairs while the other three waited inside the basement. Mason was beaming and thanking God as he zipped up the gym bag and hung it on his shoulders. Orlando was confused because Bruno didn't show any emotion at all. He just stared at him with cold, empty eyes. He didn't know what the problem was, but he was positive one existed. He figured whatever it was about couldn't be too serious. They had just hit a lick and money was the answer to everything. It was a sweet payday. No problems. No mistakes. Easy as taking candy from a baby.

Before Poncho exited the house to get WhichAway, he helped himself to some barbecue burgers and hot dogs sitting inside the aluminum pan on the kitchen table. Mason wasn't the only one to notice the food. Poncho was a rich man now. He deserved a tasty treat, so he dug in. The first bite had his taste buds holy dancing across his tongue. The second bite was like tasting a piece of heaven. The third bite was interrupted by the kitchen lights suddenly turning on. He turned around with a mouth full of burger, expecting to find his partners. Instead, he came face to face with a shirtless, muscular man wearing a pissed off mug on his face. The man stood aggressively in front of him holding a Louisville slugger baseball bat.

"What the hell are you doing in my house?" he growled.

For a split second, Poncho froze, scared shitless. The coaster went down.

"What the hell was that?" Mason asked Bruno.

There were loud noises coming from upstairs. It sounded as if people were playing tackle football inside the house. The Locos pulled out their guns and ran with urgency up the stairs, taking two steps at a time. When Bruno opened the door, he saw Poncho being thrown around the kitchen like a rag doll by some muscular cock strong cat.

"Get this motherfucker off me!" Poncho screamed once he realized his Locos were there.

The man turned towards the group of teenagers; eyes filled with combat. Bruno didn't hesitate. He squeezed the trigger five times, sending piercing hot metal through the man's chest. He crashed through the kitchen table, landing flat on his back. Barbecued meat went flying everywhere. The ape of a man wasn't dead yet. He grabbed the stovetop, on instinct alone, pulling himself up from the floor. Bruno stuffed the empty gun in his pocket then picked up the Louisville slugger baseball bat laying on the floor. As the wounded man fought to get his legs to cooperate with his body, Bruno cracked a home-run to the side of his face. Broken teeth flew from his mouth, slamming up against the wall like a pair of dice in a trap house crap game. He crashed down face first on the floor. His body violently shook and twitched uncontrollably. Mason spazzed out, believing the man was transforming into some kind of undead zombie. He panicked and fired four bullets in the back of the monster's head. One last deep breath, then nothing. The monster was dead. The Locos looked at each other, all realizing at the same time what to do next. They ran faster than a Muslim from a Klu Klux Klan rally. The side of the dead man's head was caved in.

Dark Alabama Crimson Tide colored blood was splattered all over the kitchen. His brown eyes were crossed, forever frozen into eternity. His face, once the color of a hot cappuccino, was now the color of a bedsheet. It started off as a burglary that turned into a home invasion and escalated quickly into a senseless homicide. The wheels of fate were rolling.

SIXTEEN

The high Poncho rode last night after tasting his piece of the American Pie was blown because of a nightmare fueled by images of blood and homicide. The scene on King Hill... he would never forget. A hardcore horror flick came to life. He witnessed a man die. No, scratch that. He witnessed a man's murder, and he was a part of it. His hands were just as dirty as Bruno and Mason's. The Locos weren't just a group of kids anymore. They were a gang. A small gang, but still a gang. He wondered if God forgave killers, or if by killing someone his fate would be to die by the hands of some other killer. One thing he knew for sure, Bruno was in charge. He was John the Baptist leading them to the water, baptizing them in a lake of fire. It was what it was. What will be, will be. The upside was that he had a pocket full of bread. Four thousand racks to be exact. That was his cut of the cash. He had a lot more coming once Bruno asked Big to help him flip the dope. Poncho's baller dreams were finally coming true. Maybe murder wasn't such a bad thing. Maybe it was just one of those things that came with success. You got what you put in. All or nothing. He wondered if he was going to hell. Thou shall not kill. He wondered if he was going to prison. A man was murdered. He wondered if they were one in the same. He thought about how WhichAway dropped them off last night at Bruno's crib. After they split up the bag filled with one-hundred-dollar bills, Bruno confronted Orlando. He was serious about his dough, but he was crazy over Savannah. Orlando had called Savannah a bitch while they were downstairs in that basement over on King Hill. As Orlando was trying to tell everyone to keep quiet about what happened on King Hill, Bruno bitch slapped him in the mouth.

"Damn, bruh! What's wrong with you?" Orlando asked in shock.

"My girl's name is Savannah! Not bitch, ho, freak or none of that shit."

"So, you wanna bump over a bitch?" Orlando said.

Bruno threw five hard punches at Orlando's face, and all five landed. Orlando threw a wild haymaker back but missed. That's when Mason and Poncho jumped in, serving an old-fashioned beat down on their brother Orlando. He ended up with a black eye and a couple of lumps on his head, nothing major. They weren't trying to kill him; he just needed a reality check. Locos don't accept disrespect, and nobody raises a hand to Bruno. Nobody. He was their leader, the head dog in charge. Once Orlando stopped trying to fight back, they eased up off him. Slowly, Orlando staggered to his feet. Bruno hugged him in a brotherly embrace.

"You my bruh to the grave and on my mama I'm willing to kill for you, but she means somethin' to me, bruh. She's mine," Bruno said. "Respect it."

Orlando, still shaking off the cobwebs inside his head, hugged him back clumsily. "I know you do, bruh. Whatever you wit, I'm wit. On my mama," he slurred.

There were no hard feelings, no lingering animosity. Just an honest acceptance for the rules of the game. No use in trying to run from the money shot. Poncho's thoughts were interrupted when his mother peeked inside of the bedroom.

"Are you okay, lil man? It's almost noon and you're still in bed," she said.

"I'm good, Mami, errthang fine. It's all peaches and cream."

She had no idea how true that statement was.

SEVENTEEN

He paid for his room at the Pine Ridge Motel on Troy Highway in cash. The Middle Eastern guy working the front desk didn't even sweat him about not having an ID or driver's license. Mason pulled out a knot of one hundred dollar bills the size of Dumbo's ears. The front desk clerk asked no questions. It didn't hurt that at the age of thirteen, Mason was almost six feet tall with a voice that sounded like a young Barry White. He stretched out in the motel room's queen size bed wearing a pair of black basketball shorts. A Burger King bag filled with whoppers sat on the bedside table. He puffed deeply on a Tampa Nugget Cigar stuffed with seven grams of marijuana while Tyson Fury beat the snot out of some unknown fighter on television. The air conditioner hummed a breezy tune as he relaxed in comfort. Life was good right now. Especially without that fat bitch mother of his trying to fade his shine, always yelling and blah, blah, blah. It was never ending. He had enough bread to pay her rent for the next two years if he wanted to but damn her and the bullshit she rode in on. He didn't need her anymore. He could take care of himself now.

Yeah, a man was killed last night. It wasn't all that dramatic of a thing. Killing wasn't hard to do. It was actually kind of fun, like playing a video game, except this was real life. He didn't care because there was a little over thirteen thousand dollars in cold, hard American cash stuffed in the pocket of his jeans laying on the floor. More money than he'd ever seen in his life. Shout out to the homie Bruno. Without him, none of this would have been possible. Bruno was the golden goose that laid golden eggs. An evil-minded King Midas who hit golden licks. Even though the Locos were the same age, Mason loved Bruno like the father he never had. He felt honored Bruno asked him to watch his back while he chopped it up with Big.

"Holy shit!" Big said when Bruno unloaded the Nike gym bag's contents on the kitchen table.

Big placed each Ziplock bag on a scale, minus one bag of marijuana they'd given WhichAway for driving them to and from King Hill. The remaining bags of marijuana weighed a pound each. The bags of cocaine held a kilo each. The young Locos had hit a big boy lick. Big was impressed and made Bruno an offer he couldn't refuse. Forty thousand dead presidents for everything. That equaled to ten grand a piece for each Loco plus the sixteen thousand they split up last night. Giving each Loco a grand total of fourteen thousand dollars. Big confiscated both guns used in the murder and told Bruno he'd get rid of them for him. He replaced the dirty heaters with two clean nine-millimeters. One for Bruno and one for Mason. He told them they were like sons to him, and they were on their way to greatness. He promised he would do whatever it took to make sure they developed properly out here in these streets. Mason finally felt as if his life had a purpose. After he and Bruno hand-delivered Orlando and Poncho's share of the loot, the two young Locos parted ways for the evening. Mason hit Burger King up then rented a motel room for the next couple of weeks. Bruno headed over to his precious Savannah's crib. As Mason laid on the motel's comfortable bed high as the moon and stars, he drifted off into a deep sleep. The nine-millimeter was clutched tightly in his left hand as a half-eaten whopper with cheese laid peacefully across his chest.

Yeah, life was good.

EIGHTEEN

There's nothing like drugs, booze, and hoes to help a kid get pass his problems. Orlando definitely had problems going on in his life. Lucky for him, his cousin WhichAway provided a means for escape. Orlando hadn't slept since the homicide on King Hill. His stress level was through the roof. He felt as if the police were going to swoop down on him at any moment and deliver him into the merciless arms of so-called justice. WhichAway promised him that he had the perfect remedy to take the edge off. Something to make him enjoy the moment instead of stressing over it. He rented a room at the Diplomat Inn on West South Boulevard. The room was stocked with high grade marijuana, cocaine, cases of liquor, orange juice and four dusty slut buckets he knew from the Trenholm Court Housing Projects. These low life whores were notorious freaks. Their names were Belinda, 18 years old, Mattie, 17 years old, Dottie, 16 years old, and Samille, 15 years old. These were not your typical teenage boppers. They arrived ready and willing to commit every carnal sexual sin listed in the Sodom and Gomorrah book of twisted fornication. These whores were hardcore freaks with the sexual experience of a worn-out prostitute in an Atlantic City Cat house. They had the morals of a dead lizard decomposing in the gutter. Virtue was a word they knew nothing about. These Northside project thots wore matching wardrobes that consisted of a whole lot of nothing, leaving nothing to the imagination. Orlando liked them. He liked them a lot. They kind of reminded him of his mother. That was a creepy thought to have in the middle of such animal lust. But his mind wasn't working properly. This was the first time he ever snorted cocaine. The liquor and marijuana didn't help. It only led him deeper down that black hole, leaving his mind in the midst of a geeked up drunken stupor. As he fought within himself to gain composure, WhichAway was suffering from a spell of loose lips. He couldn't stop talking about the lick on King Hill. Bragging about how much money and dope the Four Locos rode off with in a pathetic attempt to impress his female friend.

"I ain't goin' into details, but Orlando had to murk a fool last night. He's young, but he'll turn up quick. Ain't that right, lil cuz?"

Orlando didn't respond. He was zoned out. Stuck in space without a clue.

"Is that how he hurt his face?" Samille asked, turned on by all the talk of money, murder and drugs.

"He claims Four Locos on the Southside," WhichAway said. "A couple bruises and bumps ain't shit. This Lil Loco is all about that murk game."

"Is that how it is, Lil Orlando? You 'bout that Murk game?" Samille asked, licking her lips seductively. Orlando still didn't respond. He was stuck on the bed, unable to move. Frozen like an image on a photograph.

"Gurl, he's one of them quiet, dangerous types. I like that," Dottie said as she sat beside him while Samille sat on his other side.

Without warning, Samille stuck her tongue so deep in his mouth, you would've sworn it was some prehistoric baby making ritual taking place before your eyes. Dottie unzipped his fly and massaged his teenage throb to the point of near explosion. Within a few minutes, the skimpy clothes the girls wore were tossed on the floor. Nothing but naked bodies and anticipation filled the room. Fueled by the effects of the cocaine, Orlando looked Samille in her drunken eyes and dug deep into her flower bed. She devoured the few remaining pieces of innocence that he had left. It was dirty. It was obscene. It was unnatural and without any emotional attachment. It was perfect. There is nothing like drugs, booze, and hoes to help a kid get past his problems. Orlando, the bastard son of a pimp and his bottom bitch, was being rewarded with reckless, unprotected group sex for his participation in a homicide. Martin Luther King Jr. rolled over in his grave. Jesus wept.

NINETEEN

A piping hot, large, Pizza Hut pepperoni pizza with extra cheese sat between Savannah and Bruno on the bed. Morray's song "Quicksand" was bumping out of the radio box. Aunt Pam was in her bedroom filling up on premium diesel fuel. Bruno knew what floated her boat. Two cases of ice-cold Budweiser and she had no objections with him being there. She kept out of sight, out of mind. That was the point.

Savannah had no idea the Locos had robbed the crib in King Hill. Bruno figured it was better to keep her in the blind. He didn't know how she would feel about what happened. Hell, he didn't even know how he felt about it. Besides, they were enjoying their night together. Details about a man that got murdered would definitely blow the vibe. Savannah went to the kitchen to grab a couple of chilled Dr. Peppers for them to wash down their food. While she was out, Bruno worried about what kind of shit he'd gotten himself into. Nobody was supposed to be in that crib on the Hill, but there he was. They'd jerked dude around bad. Real bad. So what? It was just his time to go. If it was meant for him to live, he would've lived.

God works in mysterious ways. That's what his grandmama used to say before she died. No matter how you try to put a spin on it, everybody dies at one point or another. Some die by natural causes, others by gunshots. To live is to experience death. No way of avoiding it.

What the hell was up with Poncho? Poncho should've killed that nigga from the beginning. Then there was Orlando standing there with his mouth open like a catfish on the end of a bamboo fishing pole. Spooked. And he had the balls to call Savannah Parker a bitch. If it wasn't for her, they'd all still be slouching around at home, broke as a joke. Of course, he had to lay hands on Orlando. Savannah was his girl. She was his destiny. She belonged to him. Speaking of Savannah, where was she? What was taking her so long to come back with those sodas? She must have been making them from scratch. Anyway, Thank God for Mason Monroe. He was down for whatever. His trigger finger stayed hungry for action. He was built for this shit. The Locos were going to make a lot of bread together. That he was sure of. They were his brothers, and he would protect them. He would keep them all alive. He promised himself that.

Again, he thought, *Where the hell is Savannah at?* He laid his half-eaten slice of piping hot pizza back in the pizza box. Then he went to find out what was taking so long. When he walked into the living room, there she was holding a cold soft drink in each hand. She was standing in front of the television with her back to him.

"Wassup, girl, you must've forgot about me?"

She didn't respond, move or anything. She just stood there paralyzed like she had a devastating spine injury.

"I'm starting to get lonely back here by myself," he said jokingly.

Still, she didn't say a word or move an inch. He was about to say something when he realized what held her attention hostage. There was a news reporter on the television finishing up a breaking news report. The reporter was standing in front of the crib on King Hill.

"The community is in shock about the murder that took place here on Mary Jane Avenue last night," the reporter said.

An old woman who lived across the street appeared on the television screen.

"I've been living in this neighborhood for twenty plus years. I've known Alberto and his younger brothers since they were kids playing over there in their grandmother's yard. He was well-mannered, respectful, made good grades in school and joined the military after he graduated. His murder was senseless and whoever did this needs to be caught and given the death penalty."

The news reporter appeared back on the television. "The police are actively investigating this heinous crime. If you have any information, please call Crime Stoppers at 334-265-2111."

"Look, Savannah, I can explain," he pleaded.

"What happened?" she asked in a deep trance. However, she already knew the answer to her own question. Bruno had murked the man they were talking about on television, and she knew it was all her fault.

Bruno confessed to her everything that happened from beginning to end. Every gruesome detail. Little good that did. He didn't feel relief by getting it off of his chest. It was the opposite. He felt like Savannah wanted to get as far away from him as possible.

"I understand if you don't want me to come around no more," he said.

"I don't want you to ever leave me, Bruno!" she said desperately with tears running down her cheeks.

"I ain't gon' leave you, Savannah. Not ever." He hugged her tightly, afraid that if he let her go, she would change her mind.

"Bruno, I'm scared." Her voice was an anguished whisper.

"Everything's gon' be alright. I promise." His voice dropped to a caressing whisper. "I love you, Savannah."

Her head lay against his chest, comforted by his soothing words and tight embrace.

She whispered, "I love you too, Bruno."

She meant it just as much as he did, if not more. The young couple had surrendered their hearts to one another. They were in love. Dangerously in love. Even if all roads lead to the darkest pits of hell, they'd be together. She belonged to him, and he belonged to her.

TWENTY

Her oldest child. The one who taught her how to be a mommy. The one who taught her it was possible to love another human being more than she loved herself was dead. Three weeks had passed since she buried him. Three days since she attempted to put some food in her stomach. Four hours since she tried to overdose on sleeping pills. Ashes to ashes. Dust to Dust. She would never see her baby's face again in this lifetime. She lay broken on a bed of despair, locked inside of her lonely bedroom with the curtains closed, shutting out the outside world. She would never again hear his voice or laugh at another one of his corny jokes. The hurt was too much to bear. Day after day, night after night, she just wanted to fade away and die. Alfonso had no clue what to do to ease her pain. His older brother was gone. His little brother was engaged in a life of crime. His mother, mentally null and void. Life had been flipped upside down. Turned to shit in about as long as it takes to pull the trigger on an illegal firearm. He wanted to lay on his bed and cry all day too, but he couldn't do that. He had to be strong for his family's sake. It's what Big would've wanted.

Everything was falling apart. It couldn't get any worse. He felt like choking up. "No need for tears," he told himself. "Crying doesn't fix anything. It only leaves you looking like a pussy."

Boom! Boom! Boom!

Somebody was knocking on the front door. He didn't feel like answering, but he got up and did it anyway. His big homie, Larry O, was standing on the porch with his sister. Even though Alfonso had booty called her on multiple late nights in the past and Larry O was his mentor and best friend, he wasn't excited to see either of them.

"What up, Money Gang. How ya folks doin'?" Larry asked.

"They holdin' on as good as can be expected. What the deal is?"

"Well, my lil sister told me some shit 'bout yo' brother I think you should know."

"Oh yeah? Go on, spit it out then, Mattie."

"First, I just wanna say I'm sorry 'bout Albert . He ain't deserve to die like that."

"Yeah, I appreciate it, but just get to the point," Alfonso said, getting irritated. This bitch was always up to something. Always searching for an angle to benefit her own personal objective. Always with a trick up her sleeve.

"You ain't gotta be so mean about it. Anyway.... The night your brother got murked, me and my homegirls were kicking it with these two kids at the Diplomat Inn. They were bragging about how they just robbed and murked some guy the night before. They were talking about how they made a come up on a bunch of money and dope. So, in my mind, I'm like hell nah 'cause I ain't never heard of Big selling no dope. But the thing is, I ain't heard 'bout nobody gettin' murked that night other than your brother. So... I dunno. I just thought... Maybe... I just thought maybe I should tell you."

Alfonso's attention was on full alert. "Who them fools is?" he asked.

"They some young boys. One of 'em name is WhichAway. I used to go to school with him. He likes to talk a lot. I mean seriously, if you tell him anything, and I mean anything, he gon' blab it to everybody. Once he starts talking, he don't know how to stop. The other one's name is Orlando. He can't be no older than twelve or thirteen. He stay in Regency Park. I dunno. But even for his age he seems kind of dangerous. Kind of like somebody you don't wanna get into it with. You know what I mean? WhichAway said he was the driver and Orlando and some other kids actually went into the house and you know. They in some lil neighborhood gang called the Four Locos."

"You know who the Four Locos is, right?" Larry asked Alfonso.

"Hell naw. Who is they?"

"Them lil dudes you served at the skating rink. They call themselves the Four Locos. Remember?"

That's when reality hit Alfonso in the face like a wet slap. *Savannah, that sneaky, ungrateful, backstabbing bitch!* Not only had she gone with him to his grandmother's house before, but she'd also been inside. On top of that, she'd actually seen him stash his work in the basement. He didn't look at her as a threat. She was just another brainless bucket. Or was she? Add in the fact that she knew the young punk ass kid he smoked, and he hadn't heard from her since. It all made sense. The pieces of the puzzle fit together perfectly. He was pissed. Blood bubbling. Trigger finger itching like it had the chickenpox.

"Where ya thoughts on that?" Larry asked.

"I believe yo' sister. Them fools killed my brother. So, now I'ma murk 'em, all of 'em."

"Well, I ain't trippin'," Mattie said. "'Cause that fool WhichAway said he was gon' pick me up the next day to take me shopping and get my hair and nails done. You think that fool showed up? Hell to the nah. I ain't heard from that fool since. So, whatever you do to that boy and his friends, he got it comin'. Ya know what I mean?"

"Yeah, I hear ya," Alfonso replied.

There was the angle. Same old tired tricks up her sleeve. Same ole Mattie. Some things never change.

TWENTY-ONE

"Just give me the money and I promise I won't shoot you," Mason said calmly with a black bandana tied around his face. His nine-millimeter was aimed at the two female cashiers standing behind the counter. The young black cashier fought not to panic while the elderly, white cashier stood frozen in fear.

"I'm giving you the money, so please don't hurt us," the black cashier pleaded.

"I already said I ain't gon' hurt y'all."

"Hurry up, fool!" Poncho shouted with a matching black bandana covering his face while standing by the front door holding a sawed-off shotgun in his hands. The black chick put the money in the plastic bag and handed it to Mason. He looked behind the counter at her lovely lady lumps.

"Nice ass," he said then shot her in it. She fell to the floor holding her left butt cheek and screaming like she'd been shot in the ass when in reality, she had been. Mason jumped across the counter and grabbed as many cartons of cigarettes the plastic bag could hold.

"Why are you doing this?" the elderly white cashier cried out.

Mason slapped her in the face so hard with the handgun that her dentures flew out of her mouth and shattered on the floor. He secured his bag of loot and fled the gas station. Poncho followed him. The two Locos hopped in the back of a stolen car. Big floored the gas pedal, speeding off into the sunset.

"Three hours and thirty-four minutes. That was twenty minutes and five seconds faster than yesterday's time," Big said, looking at his watch. "Poncho and Mason are the winners."

For the last couple of weeks, Big had been schooling the young Locos on what he thought every street hustler should know how to do. The first thing he taught them was how to drive a car and how to hot wire one. After they caught on to that, he taught them how to commit a strong-armed robbery. The Locos ate up everything he taught them. They were fast learners. They wanted to prove themselves to their teacher, so Big split them up on teams. The first team was Bruno and Orlando. The second team, Mason and Poncho. The competition was to see what team could rob ten consecutive gas stations in the shortest amount of time. Orlando and Bruno had gone the day before, completing their robbery spree twenty minutes and five seconds longer than it had currently taken Mason and Poncho to complete theirs.

"You didn't have to shoot that lady." Poncho pointed out to Mason.

"You trippin', hood. I'm Mason Monroe, the one and only one. I was born to shoot people. This is what I do. Ya feel me?"

"There's a time and place for everything, boys," Big interrupted. "A time and place for everything."

After they ditched the stolen whip and cruised back to Big's crib in Regency Park, they split the loot. After two days of strong-armed robberies, they had a combined total of ten thousand dollars and enough cigarettes to last them a year.

The Four Locos, along with Big, each got two thousand a piece.

"Ain't nobody gettin' bread like us. We in this bitch," Orlando bragged.

"I can't lie," Bruno said. "We gettin' some real cheese. Yesterday, I hit Eastdale Mall and bought Bella a bunch of Barbie dolls. I picked up my mama a perfume setup and I got my girl a couple of outfits, a pair of shoes, and a fourteen-carat gold necklace with a small sparkly diamond hanging on it. My folks good, ya feel me?"

"Money makes everything better. Get used to it 'cause y'all gon' make a lot of it," Big said with pride.

"Hey! We need to go to Looney's tonight and ball all the way out. The hood gon' go crazy," Poncho said excitedly.

"Hell yeah!" Mason said. "And we can bring some freaks back to my room and really turn up."

"I'm with it. Wassup, Bruno, you down?" Orlando asked.

"Y'all fools go ahead. I gotta spend some time with my baby tonight. Ya feel me?"

"That's wassup, hood. But we all goin' out next weekend. Even if we gotta put yo' ass in the trunk," Poncho joked.

"True that. I promise. I'll go with y'all next time."

"Bet that up hood. Tell Miss Savannah I said wassup," Poncho said.

"I'll do that. Y'all fools be up and stay strapped."

Bruno dapped up Big and his Loco brothers. Then he headed home to play the good son for a little while before easing his way over to Savannah's crib.

TWENTY-TWO

"Oh my God! It's sooo beautiful!" Mia said, admiring the diamond necklace on Savannah' neck.

"Bruno gave it to me yesterday with two Guess jean outfits and a pair of Jordans with pink laces."

"Are you serious? Lil Bruno ballin' like that? Where he gettin' all this money from?"

"I dunno. He don't like me asking questions like that so I don't."

"You got a real one, gurl. You better hold on to him."

"I mean... like duh." Savannah giggled.

"You know what? Y'all should have a baby so I can be an auntie."

"Baby? Oh my God, you're..."

Savannah was interrupted by a green Cadillac pulling up and parking in front of her crib. A wave of fear surged thru her body. She knew exactly who it was. She'd been inside that Cadillac more times than she could count. What the hell was he doing there? It couldn't be good. She hadn't seen or talked to him in weeks. Alfonso exited the driver's side. His younger brother Abraham got out the passenger side. They damn sure weren't there to see how she was doing. It was obvious by the expressions on their faces, these dudes were pissed.

"Wassup, bitch, long time no see," Alfonso said as he walked up and slapped the taste out of Savannah' mouth. A small stream of blood trickled down from her bottom lip. The pain was excruciating. She fought as hard as she could from crying. She lost the fight.

"Hell naw!" Mia yelled, pulling out a boxcutter from her back pocket attempting to defend her homegirl. Abraham grabbed Mia by her hair then slammed her down hard on the ground.

"Wassup, lil mama, you want some attention too?" he said, pressing the barrel of his gun to the side of her head.

Alfonso wrapped his hands around Savannah' throat, squeezing so hard that her eyes were bulging from their sockets. No matter how desperately she tried, she couldn't breathe. She knew she was going to die. It was only a matter of time. As her thoughts became cloudy and the world around her began to fade, Alfonso released his grip. She fell to the ground, violently choking, coughing and gasping for air. He shoved his gun into her open mouth and made her deep throat the barrel over and over again until her gag reflex kicked in, causing her to puke all over herself.

"You listen real good to what I'm tellin' you. The next time ya lil Loco boyfriend come over here, you call me and let me know. If you don't call me or try to save him, the next time I see you, I ain't gon' be so gentle. Ya understand?"

Unable to talk, she nodded her head.

"Now you bein' the good lil bitch I remember," he growled then kicked her in the stomach. Abraham walked up and stood over her as she lay on the ground in agony.

"If it was up to me, you'd be dead, Savannah," he said then spit in her face.

The message had been delivered loud and clear. The Money brothers got back in the Cadillac and sped off down the street.

TWENTY-THREE

After two hours of playing Barbie dolls with Bella, Bruno was exhausted. If it was up to his little sister, they would be playing with dolls all day, every day. Thank God she was just as worn out as he was and had fallen asleep in the midst of her new Barbie doll collection. After gently picking her up off the floor and laying her down on her twin-size bed with the My Little Pony comforter, he watched her as she slept. He loved his little sister to death. She was truly an angel. He laughed at the thought of what she'd said earlier when he told her she needed to find some little girls to play dolls with.

She said, "*You a lil gurl, so I wanna play with you.*" Bruno laughed.

He said, "*Ok, Miss Smart Mouth. I'll play with you, but don't ever tell anybody I'm a lil girl. Deal?*"

"*Okay, Bruno, I won't tell. So, can we play now?*"

God, he loved her. As she lay there asleep on the bed, dreaming about butterflies and tootsie rolls, he crept out of her bedroom. His mother was in the bathroom taking a hot shower. He called her from outside of the door.

"Mama, I'm 'bout to go."

"Where are you going?!" she shouted back.

"Over to Savannah's house."

"I ain't surprised. You've been spending a lot of time over there lately. When am I going to meet this girl?"

"Soon, Mama, I promise."

"It better be soon, and don't be out too late. Tomorrow's a school day."

"Ok. Bella is in her bed asleep. I'll be back before it gets too late."

"Alright, baby boy. Be safe. I love you."

"I love you too, Mama."

In no time at all, Bruno was out of the front door pedaling his Mongoose bike towards Savannah' crib. A full moon sat in the sky, observing him as he traveled up the Troy Highway. He was in a rush because the weather report predicted rain for the night, and it was already thundering and lightning. He pedaled faster. In the time it takes to hop, skip, and jump, he'd pulled up in front of Savannah' crib. Mia was sitting on the porch talking on a cordless phone.

"I gotta call you back," she said as Bruno walked up.

"What's up, Mia, how's it hangin'?"

"Alfonso lookin' for you," she said flatly.

"Why you say that?"

Mia told him everything that had happened with the Money brothers. Afterwards, she felt an ill chill rush through her tiny frame. She sensed something bad simmering beneath the surface. This wasn't the same Bruno she'd grown up with. There was now something kind of dark and menacing about him. As she stood with him on the front porch, she noticed his eyes were cold. So cold she could read nothing in them whatsoever.

"Where's Savannah?" he asked grimly.

"She's in her bedroom, but she's messed up Bruno. We

thought they was gon' kill us. She won't even talk to me. I think she's in shock or something."

Bruno didn't respond. He walked inside the trailer and into her bedroom. She was sitting on the bed with her knees curled up to her chest, staring aimlessly out of the window.

"Are you okay?" he asked. She lowered her face to her knees. "Savannah, I...I'm sorry." He touched her arm, but she only curled herself into a tighter ball of defense. He sat down beside her and draped his arm over her shoulder. "I know this is my fault. I should've been here to protect you, but it ain't over. I promise you that.

Savannah lifted her head and looked into Bruno's eyes. They were dark and sorrowful.

"This is gonna end bad, ain't it?" she whispered.

"It's gon' end tonight. That's a promise." He kissed her softly on the lips and stood up to leave.

"Where ya goin', Bruno?"

"Just know that I love you."

As he opened the bedroom door to leave, Savannah asked him, "What you gon' do?"

A flush of raw anger hit him when he thought about what they'd done to her. "Just know that I love you." He closed the bedroom door behind him.

Mia was sitting Indian style on the couch in front of the muted television set. She'd heard everything said in Savannah' bedroom.

"You stayin' over here tonight?" he asked her.

"Yeah, I'll stay."

"Good." He turned to leave.

"Bruno?" Mia said unexpectedly.

"What up?"

"Be safe, bruh-in-law."

"Alright, sis," he said, and he was gone.

TWENTY-FOUR

Gucci Man's song "Members Only" was thumping through the speakers inside of Looney's Skating Rink. Thugs were grinding on freaks; freaks were grinding on playas and dykes were grinding on each other. Mason, Poncho and Orlando were being treated like ghetto royalty. They were all rocking big dumb gold chains, gold nugget earrings, flashy three finger rings and expensive gold watches with matching bracelets. The trio of young Locos were all wearing black jeans and Nike Bo Jackson sneakers The only thing that separated them from each other were the baseball jerseys they wore. Orlando wore a Chicago White Sox jersey, Mason wore a Pittsburgh Pirates jersey, and Orlando sported a New York Yankees jersey.

The young Locos were fresh to death and stood out like a pregnant chick at a pro-choice rally. All the hustlers wanted to be affiliated with them and all the freaks wanted to freak them. The scene belonged to the Locos. While Mason and Poncho were talking to a group of girls, Orlando was hugged up and sharing an eight ball of cocaine with Samille in a dark corner of the skating rink. Ever since they had that threesome at the motel a few weeks ago, they'd been hooking up on the regular. He was beginning to develop feelings for her which spooked him because basically, she was a slut bucket. However, he figured his mother was one too so what the hell.

"That's that good shit," Samille said, wiping away some leftover cocaine residue from her nose.

"Only the best for you, pretty girl," Orlando replied.

"I bet you tell all the girls that."

"Nah, only the ones I'm fuckin'."

They started kissing. Her tongue tasted like alcohol and cigarette smoke. She stuck her hand inside of his pants and stroked his Magic Johnson with slow, perpetual motion.

"You like that baby?" she asked as Orlando closed his eyes and leaned his head back against the wall.

There were fireworks going off inside of his skull. Her strokes became faster and with less gentleness. It was intense, too intense. His future children felt as if they were coming prematurely. He wanted to make her slow down but couldn't. He'd been temporarily paralyzed by the touch and feel of her talented fingers, so he gave up, deciding to go with the flow. Just as he was about to flow all over himself, she stopped. He couldn't believe she just quit like that. Right at the moment when he was about to explode. What the hell was her problem? You don't do that kind of thing to a man. Her mother should've taught her better.

"The hell you stop for?" he asked, obviously irritated.

"Calm down, Ron Jeremy. It's about to go down with ya homeboys and Abraham 's crew over there," she said, pointing a manicured nail over to the other side of the skating rink.

Mason and Poncho were squared off with Abraham and his entourage. Both sides were barking. Neither side appeared to be backing down. Orlando pulled himself together and made his way over to the scene with Samille right beside him.

"So y'all fuck boys thought this shit was sweet, huh? Thought you was gon' murk my brother and nothin' was gon' happen to ya! I'm 'bout that life, coward! All y'all team some bitches."

Abraham was looking for an excuse to spray bullets. Any excuse. All they had to do was give him one.

"You trippin', bruh. We ain't got no problem with you. You got us mixed up with somebody else," Poncho said.

"Y'all the Four Locos, ain't ya? So, how the hell, I got you mixed up?"

Mason had his nine-millimeter on his waist. He was itching to murk this cat, but there were too many eyes watching. Orlando staggered into the circle geeked out of his mind on cocaine.

"Y'all ain't talkin' 'bout shit! This Loco Gang here, pie ass nigga!" Orlando snapped.

Abraham thought these kids were clowns. With his hand on his pistol underneath his shirt and a smirk on his face, he said, "Fuck Loco Gang, bitch ass fagot!"

Without warning, Orlando pulled an undercover .38 from his pocket. He aimed and pulled the trigger, blowing the smirk off Abraham 's face. He was dead before his body hit the ground. Kids were screaming and running for their lives as Orlando stood over the corpse and squirted four more rounds into his chest. The lights came on inside the skating rink. The DJ was ducking for cover behind the booth. Orlando was stomping Abraham 's dead body like a man who'd lost his mind. Poncho and Mason wrestled him away from the corpse.

"Come on, hood! We gotta bounce!" Poncho yelled.

That was enough to get Orlando's attention. He stuck the gun back in his pocket and the young Locos ran out of the skating rink like a fox out of a hen house. The mood was chaotic. The outcome was murder.

TWENTY-FIVE

It was a dark and dreary night. Nobody in their right mind would be outside on a night like this unless they were bums, storm chasers or on a mission of murder. Bruno had told Big what happened at Savannah' crib. Big didn't want the kid to murk someone over a broad, but he also knew there was no talking him out of it. So, instead of sending him out there alone on a suicide mission, he decided to help the youngster do it the right way.

They'd stolen an old beat-up Malibu from the Bruno's Grocery Store parking lot and the two of them crept through the night on a hunt for a Money brother. The Malibu's heater blowed like a dragon while Bruno stared aimlessly out the window. There was a sawed-off shotgun on the stolen car's floor along with a couple of boxes of shells. His pistol was under the passenger seat along with two spare magazines and a box of nine-millimeter hollow tip bullets. The chill of fear stirred at Bruno's neck. His stomach began to churn as his skin prickled with sweat. Big could feel the anxiety inside the car and knew he had to calm Bruno down.

"Hey, kid, you nervous?" Big asked, lighting a cigar.

"A little bit, I guess."

"Yeah, I remember when I was sixteen there was a gangster in the hood named Red Bull. He was a real cutthroat piece of shit. I mean really, this dude was a real dog. He was strong-arming all the neighborhood kids, taking their dope and money whenever he caught one of 'em slipping. Everybody was terrified of this dude. And I mean everybody." Big pulled on his cigar and blew its smoke into the air. "One night I was hustling real hard on the block. I had like a thousand dollars in my pocket and a half ounce of cocaine. My mama was short on the rent and needed me to come through in the clutch. No way was I gon' let her down. God rest her soul. Well, Red Bull steps down on me. He says, I either give him everything in my pocket or he gon' bust me up like a prostitute's pussy. I ain't never been that scared in my life. I ain't want no problem with this nigga, but a problem was all he had to offer." He drew in smoke and sighed it out again.

"What happened?"

"Well, I pulled out an old rusty long nose .38 I stole from my granddaddy and lit that bitch up like the 4th of July. He was the first man I ever killed. From then on, I had respect in the hood. Dudes knew I wasn't sweet. If they thought about trying me, they knew they would have to kill me or die 'cause I was damn sure willing to kill them. Alfonso is your Red Bull. What you gon' do, youngster?"

Bruno looked Big dead in the face with eyes colder than a Colorado winter. "I'ma kill that motherfucker," he said with murder bubbling in his blood.

"That's a good boy," Big said, smiling. He parked the stolen car. "I'll be right here. And if something goes wrong, I got your back."

Bruno grabbed his gun from underneath the passenger seat and exited the car. He kissed the gun for luck then stuffed it inside of his jeans. Silent as night, he slipped through the shadows into the belly of the Trenholm Court Housing Projects.

TWENTY-SIX

"So, what you gon' do?" Alfonso asked Mattie as they sat on the living room couch inside of his mother's apartment.

"That's a question both of us need to answer," she said with a nasty attitude. "You know it takes two to make a baby, right?"

"Yeah, I know how it works. But you do know that birth control pills prevent babies, right?"

"I swear to God you ain't nothing, Blood," Mattie said, rolling her eyes.

She'd taken a pregnancy test earlier that day and found out she'd gotten knocked up. A helpless baby was the last thing in the world she wanted. But at least it would give her some financial gain with the child support and all.

"Listen, Mattie. Your brother Larry is like a father to me. So, on the strength of him, I'll take care of you and the baby."

His words put a smile on her face as she picked up her tall can of beer off the living room table and took a big gulp. Mattie was a textbook hoodrat. Meaning, whatever reason made a gangster like Alfonso Money claim her unborn baby without a blood test was looked upon from Mattie's point of view as nothing other than a blessing.

"I'ma hold you to that," she said, grinning from ear to ear.

"I bet you will," he replied.

The telephone in the kitchen started ringing. Alfonso got up from the couch and answered it on the fourth ring.

"What up?"

Whoever it was on the other end didn't say anything, but he could hear them breathing into the phone.

"Who is this?" he asked, beginning to get irritated.

"Uh...It's me... Savannah," she said nervously.

"Bitch, do you know what time it is?!" he snapped. "Why you callin' so late?"

"I thought you wanted me to call when Bruno was over here?"

"He over there now?"

"No, but he'll be here in a minute."

"Alright. He don't know you talked to me, do he?"

"No, he don't know nothin'. Can you just promise me you won't kill him?"

"Bitch, I ain't gotta promise you nothin'. Just be thankful I ain't gon' kill yo' schemed out ass. You understand what I'm sayin'?"

"Yeah, I understand," she whispered.

"Good. When he get over there, I want you to leave yo' front porch light on and unlock the back door."

"Okay... but-"

Alfonso hung up the phone in her face. He felt a surge of adrenaline rush through his veins. It was time to avenge his older brother's murder. It was the only thing that would give him closure. With a glance at his watch, he made a phone call.

"What's up, Larry O? You sleep?"

"Nah, I'm just chillin' wit my girl. What up?"

"I got a drop on one of them Loco kids. Time to lay down some murder music. Is you singin' wit me?"

"Yeah, we can do somethin'."

"True that. Look, I got ya sister over here. We can drop her off at ya mama's house on the way."

"Sounds good."

"So, just meet me in the parking lot. We'll take my car."

"Cool. I just gotta throw on some clothes, and I'll meet you there."

"Bet."

After Alfonso hung up the phone, he noticed Mattie watching him from the doorway.

"What kind of bullshit you and my brother got goin' on?" she demanded.

"Hold up, Mattie. If me and you gon' work out, you ain't gon' get in my business, ever. Now go get ya shit. We 'bout to drop ya ass off at ya mama's house."

Mattie spun around on her heels, madder than cow disease, snatched her purse off the couch and stormed out the front door. This broad was five miles past getting on his fucking nerves. He cursed himself for being careless by not wearing a condom. However, now wasn't the time to dwell on that. He had bigger fish to fry over on the Southside of town. He secured the pistol on his waistline and followed Mattie through the front door.

Outside, it was eerily quiet. Other than the half-assed drops of rain sounding on the concrete, there was nothing. Just the kind of dead silence that lives at night and only in Alabama. As Alfonso and Mattie walked towards his Cadillac, she was still cursing, ranting and raving. So much that neither of them noticed the masked gunman that stepped out of the shadows. As Alfonso dug in his pocket for the key to unlock the driver's side door, he and Mattie were assaulted with a flurry of gunshots.

Alfonso never got a chance to return fire. When the gunman stood over him, his body was shivering and shaking on the pavement. At least one of the shots fired knocked off half of his face. Small chunks of brain matter stuck to the driver's door. Stepping over the gore that used to be Alfonso's head, he walked over to the other side of the Cadillac. Mattie had been shot once in the shoulder. She was curled up on the ground whimpering in pain. She looked up at the gunman, scared for her life. She couldn't see his face because of the black bandana he had tied around it. All she could see were his eyes. They were dark and empty. Her flesh crawled with fear as she begged for mercy.

"Please don't kill me. I'm pregnant! I won't tell on you, I swear!" she cried frantically.

He aimed the gun at her face and pulled the trigger. No more loudmouth Mattie. The shots left two golf ball size holes in the middle of her forehead. Her blood oozed into a shallow pool on the ground beneath her. He walked back to the other side of the Cadillac, stood over Alfonso, and emptied the rest of the clip into his dead body. As residents in the apartment began peeping through their window and turning on the lights inside of their apartment, the gunman disappeared into the shadows.

A large crowd gathered in the parking lot around the dead couple. The grim reaper had surely struck inside the projects, leaving its residents in total shock. Alfonso's mother ran through the crowd, wearing her robe and house slippers, wild and out of control. At that exact moment, Larry arrived on the scene. He couldn't believe what he was seeing. His baby sister and the kid he loved like his own son were lying there dead on the pavement, bodies violated by bullets. What the hell happened? This couldn't be real. He wanted to cry. He wanted to be comforted. He wanted to kill somebody. None of it made sense. He felt like he was about to have a panic attack. That's when he witnessed an image that would stain his memory forever. Alfonso's mother sitting on the ground, soaked in her son's blood, cradling his head in her arms while rocking back and forth. Her eyes told the story of a woman who was broken beyond repair. For a split second, her eyes connected with him. It was as if they were the only two people in the parking lot.

"He's gone," she cried, her voice no more than a hoarse whisper. "My baby's gone."

She let out a moan that could be heard from one side of the projects to the other. It was a sound Larry would never forget. He collapsed to the ground in tears. Moments later, Montgomery police officers, EMT, and reporters with television crews stormed the Trenholm Court projects. The victims were tagged and the body bags zipped up and loaded into the coroner's van to be taken to the morgue. By now, the police were aware of Abraham Money's murder at the skating rink. Although, at that time, none of the officers had the heart to inform the grieving mother that her youngest son had also been baptized in a violent death. The Money brothers no longer existed. Only grief and pain would stand beside their mother for the rest of her days.

TWENTY-SEVEN

At this time of night, on the streets of Montgomery, there were no red robins or blueberry-colored blue jays singing songs from Mulberry trees. There were only half-dead blackbirds with feathers darker than a tar baby's face cackling the song of death from telephone poles on the skyline's grim background. A hateful rain poured from the heavens as Savannah waited on the front porch for her soulmate to return. He had been gone for what felt like an eternity and she knew in her fragile heart that she would probably never see his beautiful face again. The gloom of the night only added to her sense of impending doom. Why did he want to be a gangster anyway? Wouldn't it have been easier to just call the police on the Money brothers and have them arrested? At least then they could've been together without worrying about Bruno trying to kill someone or someone trying to kill him. Boys were stupid like that, and there was no rhyme or reason to why they did the things they did. It was just so frustrating. She swiped away tears from her worried eyes. Thank God Mia was sound asleep. If she was awake, she'd try to comfort

Savannah and tell her everything was going to be okay. Her heart would have been in the right place, but what Savannah really needed right now was to be left alone with her thoughts of Bruno.

The night was still dreary and unnervingly quiet. Her thoughts went from bad to horrific. The stress was starting to take its toll on her. She thought she saw someone at the top of the street, though she assumed her mind was playing tricks. Suddenly, she saw it again and realized there was someone in the distance riding a bike and wearing a black hooded sweatshirt. She held her breath as the figure pulled up in the front yard and laid his bike down on its side. He walked up on the front porch and stood face to face with her while pulling his hoodie back. It was Bruno. At that precise moment, there was no doubt in her mind that God answers prayers. He leaned down and kissed her trembling lips softly and thoroughly. Her knees went weak, causing her to cling to him for balance. She looked into his eyes and saw pure, unconditional love.

"Is it over?" She gave him a pleading look.

"Yeah. It's over," he said then kissed her again.

Holding hands, they walked inside of the trailer and sat on the living room couch. The television was on with the volume turned all the way down.

"I called him just like you told me to," she said.

He wrapped his arm around her shoulder to draw her close to his side. "You did good, baby. Ain't nobody gon' hurt you again," he promised. Savannah couldn't stop the smile from creeping across her face. "What you smilin' 'bout?" he asked.

"I dunno. I guess part of me sees you as my knight in shining armor. Another part sees you as a gangster."

Bruno smiled as his arm tightened around her. "Whatever I am, I love you, Savannah," he said softly then kissed her. Her heart melted.

"I love you too, Bruno. I always will."

"You promise?" he asked, drowning himself in her hazel eyes and creamy skin.

For just this one moment, she wanted them to be two ordinary teenage kids in love. And that's exactly what they were. Easing over, she kissed him back.

"I promise."

There was nothing left to be said as she curled up and drifted off to sleep, cuddled inside his protective embrace. He pulled her possessively close, enjoying the smell of her hair and the feel of her warm breath breezing across his skin. He held her as if God created her specifically for him, then slipped off into the peaceful sleep of the innocent.

TWENTY-EIGHT

Bruno opened his eyes to the morning aroma of bacon frying and warm, buttery, blueberry muffins. He slept so hard he didn't even notice when Savannah awakened and left the couch. He could hear her and Mia inside the kitchen giggling and laughing. Everybody appeared to be in good spirits. Aunt Pam Strolled out of her bedroom suffering a hangover from the previous night. She noticed Bruno stretched across the couch. Her eyes flashed with annoyance.

"Bruno, do you have a home or are you living with us now?" she asked sarcastically.

"Nah, I got somewhere to live. I'm just checkin' up on my girl." He shot her an amused glance.

Savannah and Mia bopped into the living room, each carrying a tall glass of orange juice.

"Your girl? What does your young behind know about having a girl?" Pam asked.

"I know that whatever she wants, I get it for her. And my love is so good, it makes her toes curl when she thinks about me."

Bruno grinned at Savannah whose eyes were fierce and flashing him with death threats. Mia choked on her orange juice, fighting the urge to laugh.

"Uhh...You know I'm just playing, Aunt Pam," he said, smoothly changing the subject. "I appreciate you lettin' me chill over here all the time. That's why I got this for you. So you can buy yourself something nice." He pulled a crispy fifty dollar bill out of his pocket and handed it to her. Pam's face lit up like a winning slot machine.

"You're a good boy, Bruno. You're welcome over here anytime you wanna come."

"Thank you, ma'am," he responded, grinning at her choice of words.

"Alright then. Mia, make yourself useful and bring me some of those muffins and bacon to my room," Pam said as she left the living room.

Savannah pinched Bruno's arm.

"Ouch! What was that for?"

"That's for trying to play my aunt. Now get dressed and come get something to eat so we can go to school."

Bruno went into Savannah's bedroom and grabbed some of his clothes out of her closet. He threw on a pair of black Dickey pants, matching shirt, and a pair of Timberland boots. When he went into the kitchen, Savannah already had a plate of scrambled eggs, bacon, and a blueberry muffin set for him at the table. The girls stared at him with a cat's curiosity as he took a bite of his muffin.

"So, what you think?" Mia asked wearily.

"What I think 'bout what?" Bruno responded.

"About the food, you dummy," Mia said jokingly.

"Oh, it's good. Real good," Bruno stated as he stuffed a fork full of eggs into his mouth.

"We're a team," Mia said smiling. "We gon' open our own restaurant someday."

"And be richer than them white folks over in Deer Creek," Savannah said, giving Mia a high-five.

"Yeah, and I'm gon' to be y'all favorite customer," Bruno said with a mouth full of food.

After breakfast, Bruno called for a taxi to take the three of them to school since they'd missed the bus. The girls were having so much fun on the drive to school, you would've thought they were riding in a stretch limousine. Once they pulled up in front of the school and were dropped off, the trio hadn't even made it to their lockers before the shit hit the fan. A kid named Mack from Cross Creek pulled up on Bruno.

"What up, Loco Gang?"

"What up, Mack. What it do?"

"You tell me, hood. Y'all Loco boys name on fire right now. I heard 'bout ya."

"What you talkin' 'bout?" Bruno asked, completely in the blind.

"I'm talkin' 'bout Orlando, Mason and Poncho getting locked up last night for killing Abraham at the skating rink. And everybody saying you strapped up later on and murked Alfonso in Trenholm Court. That's what everybody saying."

"Oh my God," Savannah said, her eyes wide.

Mia's jaw dropped on the floor. She stood paralyzed in shock by what Mack said. Bruno's eyes were suddenly very dark and dangerous.

"So, that's what you hear, huh?" His voice was remarkably calm. "Maybe you shouldn't believe everything you hear."

Mack, realizing it would probably be in his best interest to bounce, did exactly that.

"You right, hood. I was just telling you what folks are saying. But I gotta go handle some stuff, so I'll get up with you later."

Bruno didn't respond. He felt like the walls were closing in on him. What had his Locos gotten themselves into? He couldn't wrap his mind around any of it.

"Bruno," she whispered.

He turned his attention towards Savannah. Her eyes were stormy, a hard shade of hazel, but he saw the hurt behind the fear.

"I thought you promised me it was over with," she said, sounding troubled.

"I thought it was. I don't know what these fools done gone and did."

"If the police try to lock you up, I'll tell them you ain't have nothing to do with it. You was with me and Mia the whole night."

"You ain't gon' tell 'em nothin'," he said as his dark eyes bore into hers. "Nothin'. It'll only make things worse, you hear me?"

"Yeah, I hear you." Tears filled her eyes.

Bruno had obviously hurt her feelings. He regretted it, but it couldn't be helped at that moment. Not when his entire world balanced on the brink of destruction. He paused and took a deep, steadying breath.

"Look, I don't want you to get caught up with this. Ain't no telling what's 'bout to happen. I gotta go find Big, he'll know what to do. I just need you to be my girl and hold me down until I figure out how to fix this."

Savannah folded her arms across her chest and fumed. She knew he was right, but that didn't mean she was happy about it.

"Go," she said. "You know I'll hold you down."

"I love you," he said as he cupped her face in his hands.

"I love you too," she replied, beginning to settle down.

He laid his lips on hers, soft, sweet, and innocent. "Everything gon' be okay," he promised. He pulled out a huge wad of cash, placed it in her hands, turned and walked away. As he stepped out of the front doors of Floyd Jr. High School, he was swarmed by Montgomery police Officers with their guns drawn. They slammed him face down on the ground and slipped a pair of handcuffs on his wrist.

"We have the suspect in custody," one of the police officers said into his radio.

Bruno looked up from the ground and saw Savannah standing in the entrance to the school along with Mia and a bunch of other kids and teachers. Savannah was crying, but there was absolutely nothing he could do about it. Not even twenty-four hours had passed, yet the brutal murder of Alfonso Money and Mattie had taken on mythic proportions. Even though there was no evidence or witnesses linking anyone to the double homicide in Trenholm Court, the entire inner city was gossiping about it. The suspected killer in everybody's mind was a young kid named Bruno Santana.

TWENTY-NINE

The Four Locos were being held at the Montgomery County Jail in separate cells. That way they could sweat out the multiple murders, first degree robbery and illegal possession of firearms charges. And they could sweat them out individually with no chance to corroborate each other's stories.

Homicide Detective Barry Jones and his partner Kathy Romero were preparing to interview Bruno once his mother arrived. Because he was a minor, Bruno had to have a parent or legal guardian present during questioning. They'd already interviewed Mason, Poncho and Orlando along with their parents. The detectives found the youngsters fascinating. Not only were they children, but these kids were vicious. They were real life monsters. Through the use of information given to them by an informant, they were aware that Bruno was the young Loco's leader. They were anxious to interview him and hopefully close the Money Brothers' murder case. At this point, the previous Locos didn't give them anything. So, they were banking on getting Bruno to break. After his mother finally arrived, the detectives were ready to get started.

"How are you doing, Bruno?" the detective asked.

Bruno shrugged his shoulders.

"I'm Detective Jones and this is my partner Detective Romero. We're going to record this interview and ask you a few questions, okay?"

Bruno didn't respond.

"There's been a lot of killing going on lately and your name keeps coming up in our investigations. So, we want to hear your side of the story." Detective Jones had crime scene pictures of Mattie and the deceased Money brothers on the table. "Why did all of these people deserve to die?"

Bruno's mother gasped in horror at the sight of the gory pictures. Bruno showed no emotion at all.

"At the very least, we know you were involved with this murder here." Detective Jones pointed at the picture of the oldest Money Brother, Alberto Money.

"Your buddy WhichAway told us all about how it went down. He told us he drove you and your friends to the house on King Hill to rob it. You should've never trusted him, but we're glad you did. He's a rat. A girl named Dottie handed him to us in our lap. She said he admitted to her and some other girls in some fleabag motel that he was a part of it. She also said your little friend Orlando was there as well, and he didn't deny any of it. The girl you killed in cold blood last night was her best friend. That's the reason she called us and turned WhichAway in to begin with. We picked him up a few hours ago and he sang like a bird. He wasn't willing to risk his neck to save y'all and I don't blame him. So, maybe you should tell us your side of the story before you end up on death row or spending the rest of your natural life in prison."

He studied Bruno through narrowed, objective eyes. He had calm eyes, he thought. Cold and calm. Eyes that had seen gruesome acts of violence and were immune to it.

"Listen, I already know the kid you killed last night is the same one who shot you a few months ago at Looney's Skating Rink," Detective Jones said, trying to sound sympathetic. "His brothers threatened you, so you and your friends had to kill them before they killed y'all. It was self-defense. Am I right?"

"Nice try, detectives, but the interview is over. I'm Trina Brown and I've been appointed by the State of Alabama to represent Mr. Santana as his public defender. Any questions you have in the future, I suggest you ask them to me. Are you charging him with anything?"

"Yes, we are," Detective Jones replied, obviously pissed off by the interruption. "We are charging Bruno Allen Santana with one count of murder, one count of first-degree robbery and one count of illegal possession of a firearm."

Bruno was read his rights and escorted out of the interrogation room so he could be processed into the county jail.

"Can you help my son?" Bruno's mother asked Trina with tears in her eyes.

"Well, the DA is going to want to try him as an adult, but I'm going to push to get him in Juvenile Court. I'll see what kind of evidence they have on him, and we'll go from there."

It wasn't much, but it was all Bruno's mother had to hold onto. She prayed God would protect her only son. Later that day, on the evening news, The Montgomery Police Department held a press conference.

The chief of police announced, "The purpose of this meeting is to inform the public that the suspects responsible for the murder in the King Hill community and the murder at Looney's Skating Rink have been apprehended. A group of young African American teenagers who call themselves the Four Locos are in police custody at this time. We will release more information on the continuing investigation as we receive it at a later time. Thank you."

Before it was all said and done, the entire city was familiar with the Four Locos. Some people saw them as celebrities while others saw them as common thugs. Eventually, their lawyers had their cases turned over to Juvenile Court. After months of intense negotiations between the lawyers and the State of Alabama, the Four Locos took a plea deal. Bruno, Mason, and Poncho pled guilty to one count of murder and one count of first-degree robbery. Orlando pled guilty to two counts of murder and one count of first-degree robbery. They all received the same sentence. Juvenile life plus three years. This meant they would be incarcerated in Mt. Meigs Juvenile Correctional Facility until their eighteenth birthday. Then they would be transferred to an adult maximum-security prison until they turned twenty-one. For the time being, the Four Locos were officially no longer society's problem.

THIRTY

8 YEARS LATER

"The oldest and strongest emotion of mankind is fear."
-H.P. Lovecraft

The Locos were finally finished serving their prison terms. Their childhood was officially over. They left the streets of Montgomery as children and returned to society as men with the title of ex-convict hanging over their heads. Their appearance reflected an environment they'd been incarcerated in for the last eight years. Shaved heads, skin covered in tattoos, and bodies shredded with muscles. Eight years in the Department of Corrections hadn't rehabilitated them. They evolved into hardened thugs, earned a reputation of ruthlessness and violence, and acquired the mindset of wolves while everyone else outside of the pack were simply lambs waiting to be slaughtered. It was an all gas no brakes mentality they'd picked up in the school of hard knocks. If Mason, Orlando, and Poncho graduated top of the class then Bruno was valedictorian. He was the poison between the rattlesnake's bite. Even with that being the case, in his mother's eyes, he was still her baby boy. On the drive home from West Jefferson Maximum Security Correctional Facility, she felt like she was having the most beautiful dream.

"I'm so happy you're coming home, I could shout," she declared.

"Me too, Mama. I have dreamed about this day every night since I got locked up."

"Well, it's here now and the sky's the limit for you, Bruno. What happened in the past was just a bump in the road. It's a brand new day."

"I'm ready for it, Mama."

"God's got big plans for you, boy. Me and Bella are in your corner. She's been excited all week about you coming back home."

"Yeah, Mama. It's good to be back home," he said, shaking his head.

"It really is, Bruno," she said, smiling. "It really is."

When they turned into Regency Park and pulled up at the house, Bruno felt a rush of emotions, all of them good. Before they made it to the front porch, Bella was already aware of their arrival. She greeted Bruno at the door, jumping up and down with excitement. Throwing her arms around him, she hugged him tightly and dragged him inside the house.

"Bruno! Bruno! Bruno! Oh my God! Oh my God!" she squealed.

"Calm down, baby girl," Bruno said, smiling while trying to contain his own excitement.

"I can't believe you're home," she said with tears of joy streaming from her eyes.

"Yeah, I'm home, Bella, and I ain't never leaving y'all again."

"Swear to God?"

"Yeah. I swear," he said, laughing.

"Everybody be talking 'bout y'all at my school like y'all some rap stars or something."

"Who is y'all?"

"The Four Locos stay down, four the hard way."

"Where you hear that at?"

"That's what all the Loco Gang be saying," she said, giggling.

"The fuck is a Loco Gang?"

"Bruno Allen Santana!" his mama warned from the kitchen.

"My bad, Mama," he apologized.

"Everybody on the southside claiming Loco Gang. They wanna be like y'all," Bella said matter of factly.

"Them niggas crazy," Bruno replied.

"Oh! Oh! Oh! Bruno, can you take me to the mall Saturday night? Everybody's gon' be there and they gon' go stupid when they see you," Bella said, jumping from foot to foot like an excited little kid on Christmas morning. She was full of so much energy, Bruno didn't think he could keep up with her.

It was at that point Bruno realized his kid sister was growing up. She wasn't a little girl anymore. She was a teenager who was a year older than he was when he caught his murder case. She'd grown into a beautiful, petite, dark-skinned, young girl with soft brown eyes and curly black hair. She was wearing a Coogi mini dress and a pair of thigh high boots. There's nothing permanent except for change and his sister had surely changed. *That's life,* he thought to himself. He only hoped that she hadn't given up all of her innocence. He quickly shook that thought from his head.

"Yeah, I'll take you to the mall," he promised.

"Swear to God?"

"Yeah, I swear," he said, kissing her on the cheek.

They were going to be a family again and he was going to

make sure they were properly taken care of. They rode with him during the incarceration, blessing him with unconditional love and support. He owed them. Then there was Big, the father he never had. Not only did Big deposit two hundred dollars every month for the last eight years into his prison account, but he also did the same for Mason, Orlando, and Poncho as well. They used the money to purchase food and hygiene products. They never had to beg anyone for anything, which was something Bruno would forever be grateful for. Last, but not least, there was the girl he never fell out of love with; Savannah Parker. She wrote him letters constantly for the first couple of years he was locked up, but he never responded to any of them. He knew she couldn't understand that it was impossible for him to breathe while loving her without truly having her in his life. So, he ignored her. One day, the letters stopped, and he was able to somewhat glue back together the shattered pieces of his broken heart. But he was home now, and Savannah was somewhere out there. He had to find out if there was anything left between them. If he still had a chance at happiness.

THIRTY-ONE

"The whole city has changed since y'all knuckleheads been gone," Big said, blowing a puff of cigar smoke in the air.

Bruno, Mason, Orlando and Poncho sat on the couch in his living room listening closely to each and every word that came out of his mouth. To them, Big was more than a trusted friend or a role model. He was God Almighty.

"Money being made hand over fist on every side of town. Ain't no drama between the south, north, east or west side. Not anymore. All those beefs are dead and were buried a while back. I hooked up with three shot callers from each side of town and created an organization called the Commission. There are four of us and we run the city with an iron fist. What hood you represent or what gang you're affiliated with don't mean nothing to the Commission. It's all about money, power, and respect."

Big's wife walked in the room and handed everyone a bottle of domestic beer. She was a twenty-nine-year-old, thick, redbone chick. Her name was Kesha. Bruno wondered how the old man had snatched such a bad young chick. He was impressed and like his Loco brothers, found it impossible not to stare at her with their mouth wide open. She winked at Bruno then gave Big a kiss on the cheek and left the room. Big smiled knowing these youngsters were drooling over his wife. He continued talking.

"Anyway, it ain't but four of us who sit at the table. There's Tuscaloosa Fresh on the Eastside, Larry O on the Northside, Trickshot on the Westside, and then there's me. I'm the Southside all-high, numero uno, king of the city. I get thirty percent of all the profits each month from every side of town. It's my show and what I say is law."

The Locos laughed and dapped each other up. They felt just as much pride as Big. Their teacher was on top of the game. He held the keys to the city and was the shit, which meant they were the shit as well.

"We control drugs, prostitution, gambling and extortion," Big said, putting out his cigar in the ashtray. "Everything's organized and strategically planned. No mistakes. No loose strings. I plan on bringing all of y'all into the life."

The Locos nodded their heads in agreement.

"Does this Life sound good to y'all?" he asked.

"Hell yeah!" they said in agreement.

"That means whatever I tell y'all to do, y'all do it. No questions asked."

"Hell yeah!" they said again in unison.

"That's what I needed to hear," Big said, smiling. "Now, I have a special surprise for you guys."

The Locos looked at each other with anticipation and curiosity swelling in their eyes.

"Kesha!" Big shouted. "Bring me that bag off the dresser in the bedroom."

"What's going on, Big?" Bruno asked.

"Be patient. I told you it's a surprise."

Kesha strutted into the living room like the fine thorough-bred she was and handed Big a purple Crown Royal Bag.

"Thank you, sweetie. I don't know what I'd do without you," he said, giving her perfect round bottom a playful smack. She exited the room giggling like a tickled schoolgirl.

"Y'all young knuckleheads handled your business as kids and accepted your time like real men are supposed to. I respect that about y'all to the highest. Y'all kept it real in the streets, so the streets gon' keep it real with y'all. And I am the streets. I've been waiting for y'all to come home for a long time. We gon' build and make something for ourselves out here. And this is just a little something to welcome y'all back home." Big handed each one of them a key from the purple bag. "Go ahead and enjoy your toys. They're in the backyard."

When the Locos made it to the backyard, their eyes were as big as satellites. There were four old school, custom candy painted pickup trucks sparkling like high-quality jewels parked on the lawn. After they figured out which key went to each truck, they were happier than a group of rich black men stranded on an island full of naive white women. Orlando was now the owner of a brown, deep gloss, 1959 Chevrolet pickup. Poncho had the keys to a fire engine red 1953 GMC pickup. Mason got the victory red and super black 1956 Ford 100 pickup. Bruno was blessed with the battleship gray 1953 Chevrolet 3100 pickup. Big had really looked out for them. These trucks were old school American muscle. Rotten to the core and fresh to death. Inside each truck was a manila enve-lope stuffed with five thousand dollars in cold hard cash and underneath each of the driver's seat was a glock nine-millime-ter. Christmas for the Locos had come early this year. While Mason, Poncho, and Orlando were exploring their new whips, Bruno made his way over to the back porch where Big stood like a proud papa with his arm around a giggling Kesha.

"I hope y'all like the trucks. I helped pick them out," Kesha said, tossing him a box of Trojan condoms. "Keep these on you at all times. Y'all gon' need 'em. Especially you, pretty boy," she said as Big burst out laughing.

Bruno gave her a kiss on the cheek, shook Big's hand and gave him a hug.

"I'm home, Big. Whatever you want me to do, it's done."

Big nodded his head. "Let the games begin."

THIRTY-TWO

Stick Man cruised his convertible cocaine white mustang through the Pecan Grove neighborhood. Dirty Boyz song "Hit Da Floor" was playing on his stereo. It was sunny outside. The perfect day for a barbecue. Unfortunately, Stick Man was here on business, nothing more. He pulled up and parked his whip in front of a cozy, brick, three-bedroom house with a two-car garage. He placed his gun underneath the driver's seat, walked to the front door and pressed the doorbell. A chubby, dark-skinned woman in her mid-thirties opened the door.

"Hey, baby!" she said excitedly. "Get on in this house and hug my neck."

Stick Man stepped inside, giving the woman a hug and kiss on her cheek.

"How you doin', Anita?" he asked.

"I've been good, cooking and cleaning up behind Larry O's lazy ass. You know, the usual," she said, smiling.

"Oh yea. I hear ya. But, like I told you before, you're too young to be married and messin' around wit that old geezer," he said playfully.

Anita roared with laughter. She was thirteen years younger than her husband which, in her mind, made her a youngster. Well, at least younger than him. She loved when Stick Man stopped by to visit. At twenty-three years old, he really was a youngster and always put a smile on her face.

"I'll probably just stay married to the geezer because he wouldn't be able to survive without me."

"And that, Mrs. Anita, is a fact. You truly are a saintly woman," he said, laughing. "Where's the old geezer anyway?"

"He's in the backyard. Go on out there, he'll be glad to see you. We always are."

"Thanks, beautiful," he said, giving her a kiss on the cheek.

Larry O was sitting in a lawn chair admiring his garden of watermelon plants while sipping leisurely on a glass of iced tea.

"What's up, old man? Mind if I sit with you?" Stick Man asked.

"Of course, pull up a seat," Larry O said.

"When are the watermelons gon' be ready to be picked?"

"Hell, I don't know. I just throw the seeds in the dirt and wait till they look like they do in the grocery store. Then me and Anita eat the juicy motherfuckers like two sambos in a cotton field," he said with a wolfish smile.

"Sounds like maybe you missed yo' callin' in life."

"Well, maybe in the next life. Who cares. Anyway, I know you ain't come over here to talk to me about watermelons. What's goin' on?"

"Aight, here it is," Stick Man said in a low, conspiratorial voice. "I just got word from one of my guys that Bruno is out of prison. I heard he's been back for about a week now, and that Big is working with him the long way. I mean seriously, this bitch ass nigga kills your little sister and Alfonso, and Big rewards him? Besides that, he has the balls to move back to the city like it's all good. That's some real bullshit, Larry," he said, with murder in his eyes. "All you gotta do is give me the word and I swear on all my dead homies I'll have that nigga's dead body stuffed in a dumpster before the news comes on tonight."

Larry O leaned back in his chair and took a sip of his iced tea.

"You're the only man in the game we play that I trust completely," he said, looking Stick Man in the eye. "So, I need you to trust me on the same level."

"I do," Stick Man said, nodding his head.

"Good. Because this is a chess game we're playing. Big is nothing to me but an associate. He breaks bread with a man he knows killed my flesh and blood then he smiles in my face and tells me he loves me. He knows I control the Northside and what kind of money I stuff his pockets with. That's why he keeps me in his car. But when it's all said and done, his loyalty to anything or anybody other than the Southside is gold plated. It ain't real. And neither is mine. I'm Northside 'til the death of me. So, I say let him. Big's the boss right now. Me and you, we play along for as long as it takes."

"As long as it takes to do what?" Stick Man asked.

"As long as it takes for Big to make the rest of the Commission doubt him. That's when we'll murk Big and Bruno. Then we'll take control of the Commission, and when I step down, it'll all belong to you."

Larry O took a long sip of his iced tea.

"That's actually a sweet plan," Stick Man admitted.

"Sweeter than sipping iced tea underneath the Alabama sun," Larry O said, passing Stick Man the glass of tea.

Stick Man took a deep sip. "Larry, it's more than sweet. It's delicious," he said.

Both men laughed.

THIRTY-THREE

"How much of that you gon' snort?" Poncho asked Orlando who was shoveling enough cocaine up his nose to overdose a small village. They were sitting inside of Orlando's truck in the Peabody Park parking lot. Doe B's song "Homicide" was bumping on the stereo.

"I'm tryin' to find God, hood. He's somewhere at the bottom of this bag," Orlando responded with glassy eyes.

"Good luck with that," Poncho said sarcastically. "What the hell we doin' out here anyway?"

Orlando took another bump of cocaine. "You see all them dudes over there?" He pointed to a large group of teenagers who were chilling on one of the picnic tables in the park. "They bangin' Loco Gang."

"Yeah, I heard youngsters doin' that after we got sent to the joint, but so what?"

"So what?" Orlando asked with a look on his face like he'd just been kicked in the teeth. "This our structure. We built this, and they our soldiers. Ain't nobody callin' shots in our ranks without our permission."

"You trippin'. What type of time you on, hood?"

Orlando reached underneath his seat, grabbed his Glock, and concealed it inside of his jeans.

"Watch this. I'm 'bout to show you what type of time I'm on," Orlando said as he got out of the truck.

"What the hell..."

Before Poncho could get the question out, Orlando had already closed the door behind himself. Poncho was pissed. They just got out of prison a week ago and here they were, probably about to return if Orlando did something stupid. His common sense told him to stay in the truck, but there's no way he was going to let Orlando crash out by himself. It's what it always was, Loco Gang over everything. He grabbed his Glock, chambered a bullet and got out of the truck. By the time he made it over to the picnic table, Orlando was already stepping down on the group.

"Attention family!" he shouted. "I am the Loco Gang. Me and my homeboys built this shit. Original Four Locos to the death of me. If y'all claimin' Loco Gang then y'all under the Four Locos. Respect it or check it."

The group was dead silent. Some, because they recognized Orlando and Poncho, and they were scared. The others, because they saw Orlando and Poncho with their Glocks drawn.

"Who supposed to be y'all OG?" Orlando demanded.

A light skinned guy in his early 20's with a bald head and a bunch of jailhouse tattoos stepped up.

"Here I go," he said, with forced confidence.

Orlando recognized the face but couldn't figure out from where. "I know you from somewhere. Who are you?" he demanded.

"Roscoe from Normandale. I was locked up with y'all in juvie."

It took Orlando a few seconds to remember this lame.

"Yeah, I remember you. You was burnin' hairs with them fuck niggas after lights out in the joint."

"Come on, Orlando. That was a long time ago," Roscoe pleaded.

"Come on nothin'. Ain't no chumps bangin' Loco Gang," Orlando said then spit in his face. "Yeah, that way. Get the fuck off my block."

Before Roscoe could burn out, Orlando slapped him in the face with his glock. The impact sent him to the ground, flat on his back with a broken nose.

"Please!" Roscoe screamed in terror, holding his bruised nose, trying to stop the blood from gushing.

Poncho kept his eyes and his Glock on the crowd who were watching in shock as Orlando showed them what the Loco Gang was really about. He couldn't stop himself from unleashing the violence bottled up inside of him. He slammed his fist into Roscoe's face again and again until his knuckles began to bruise and swell.

"Chill out, hood," Poncho said, seeing it was getting out of hand.

"Hell naw! I'm having fun now, hood!" Orlando shouted with insanity in his eyes.

"Come on, that fool damn near dead. Let him go."

Orlando listened to the voice of reason and got off of Roscoe. He was unconscious and blood was leaking on the ground. His face was busted; he didn't even look like the same cat anymore.

"Here's some advice, O.G. Roscoe. If you wanna be a Loco, kill yourself and pray to God that reincarnation is real so that in your next life you might be born with a set of balls, you bitch ass nigga," Orlando said then kicked him in the head and spit in his face again.

As he and Poncho left and headed back towards the truck, a kid from the group called them out.

"O.G. Orlando and O.G. Poncho!"

Both men turned around.

"Loco Gang to the death of me. We respect it, hood." Then he threw up four fingers along with the rest of the group. Poncho and Orlando threw up four fingers back. It was no longer a question to anyone who the Loco Gang leaders were. None whatsoever.

THIRTY-FOUR

After only three weeks of being released from prison, the day had arrived for Bruno's sponsorship to be announced to the Commission. He felt like he was on the fast track to reaching his goal of being king. It was now up to him how close or short he actually ended up. For this momentous occasion, he wore new Timberland boots, khaki slacks and a white button-down shirt. He wore the Glock on his waistline locked with one in the chamber. Big picked him up in his weekend car, a metallic, reef blue, 1953 Buick Skylark convertible with white wall tires. He was wearing a gray pin-striped, summer wool, custom-tailored suit, an oxford cloth cotton shirt and a burgundy silk tie. Bruno had never seen him dressed up like that before. It made him realize how important a man Big had become since he'd been incarcerated. He was beginning to feel a little nervous about his introduction to the Commission. These were more than likely the most dangerous men in the city. They controlled everything and anybody who made their living on the opposite side of the law. They were a secret society. Every move they made was done in private. Big wouldn't even tell Bruno where the meeting was being held. He was told that only the Commission and those who were being sponsored were kept in the loop. Bruno would have to be certified by all the members of the Commission before he was provided with any knowledge of their organization. He could only hope they would accept him into their private world. On their drive over to the meeting place, Bruno wanted to know more about the Commission.

"Hey, Big. Can I ask you a question?" Bruno asked.

"I'd be surprised if you didn't," he said, laughing. "What's up?"

"I was thinking about the Commission and everything, and how y'all work the shadows. So, I figured this group is somethin' like the mafia, huh?"

Big pondered his question for a moment. "Well, we are organized. We do live by a code of silence, and we don't discuss business with outsiders. We are a commission of hustlers who believe in maintaining order, protecting our own, and enforcing our rules in the street. If that's what you consider the mafia, then more power to you."

"So, you trust these men with your life? You know what I mean, like how I trust you and the Locos?"

"Listen, Bruno. Be careful how you throw around that trust word. It's dangerous and usually the cross-game travels with it. You dig what I'm saying? Always watch for the cross. It's always there and ain't no hustler safe from it. Hell, even Jesus died on the cross. He was out there hustling souls and his own disciple set him up for the kill. If a motherfucker would betray Jesus then you know a motherfucker would betray you. The reason most folks don't see it coming is because their enemies come disguised as their friends and loved ones. I mean, everybody is suspicious of rivals and strangers. That's a given. But most folks don't expect their friend, brother or main squeeze to be the one to stick that knife in their back. That's why most folks ain't prepared to defend against it. In this life we live, you gotta always walk with your head up and your eyes wide open. Don't ever overlook nobody. It don't matter if they're your friends, wife, me or even one of your Locos. The minute you trust anybody other than yourself absolutely, you're dead."

Bruno took those words to heart.

As they drove down a country county road on the outskirts of Montgomery, Big turned left down a long gravel driveway which led to a small dingy white, single-wide trailer where a group of luxury cars were already parked. He cut off the engine.

"Well," he said. "Let's get the show started."

The first thing Bruno noticed when they entered the trailer was a large, mahogany, round table with three older men sitting around it in rich brown padded leather chairs. They resembled the stereotypical mob bosses except they were African American men and preferred fried chicken over spaghetti and meatballs. They wore expensive European suits, and all of their heads were invaded with gray hair. Cigarettes and Cuban cigars hung from their lips while thick white smoke consumed the room. There were large oil paintings on the walls of famous African American leaders throughout history. The smell of burnt tobacco, expensive cologne, and Head Shop incense mixed together to create a fragrance that Bruno decided was pure gangster. Behind each of the older men stood a young man. These dudes carried all business, no games expressions on their faces and they all kept a hand tucked underneath their shirts. On a first impression one would think that they were bodyguards, which was true. But these men were also being groomed to be the next in line to hold the positions of the older men that each of them stood behind. Big took his seat at the head of the table, then motioned Bruno to stand behind him. When in Rome, one does as the Romans do, so Bruno clutched the Glock he had underneath his shirt. As he looked around the room, he saw that all eyes were on him, and they weren't friendly.

"Everybody good?" Big asked. "This is Bruno Allen Santana. He's out of Regency Park. I've known him since he was a kid and I take full responsibility for him. He takes care of business and keeps his mouth shut. He also knows the rules to the game we play and the consequences that come along with breaking the rules. I sponsor him in this life of ours and officially label him as certified."

There was an intense silence inside the trailer as everyone stared so hard at Bruno that he felt like they were looking into his soul to see if there were any signs of bitch dwelling in him. After a short, intense moment that seemed more like an eternity Tuscaloosa Fresh broke the silence.

"He is certified."

"Yeah, he's certified," Trick Shot agreed.

Larry O took a long drag from his cigar, filling his lungs with smoke. He exhaled slowly, never breaking eye contact with Bruno. If given the green light, Stick Man was ready to body Bruno right then and there.

"He's certified," Larry O finally agreed.

Big smiled. "Then it is an agreed majority. Bruno's my new number two. Now let's get down to business."

The older men gave their proteges standing behind them the signal to leave the trailer. Bruno followed suit and left Big to discuss business with the Commission. He felt more excitement rushing through his body. He felt proud and honored that Big allowed him to be a part of the organization. He swore to himself that he would never cause his mentor to regret his decision. The young men chilled outside and lit up their blunts of fruity.

"What it do, Bruno. I'm Jay Spray, I ride with Trick Shot. This here is Willie Black, he rides with Tuscaloosa Fresh, and that's Stick Man, he rides with Larry O. Welcome to the circle."

Bruno shook hands with each one of them. Stick Man watched him like a hawk.

"What's the circle?" Bruno asked.

"Damn, homie, you don't know what the circle is?" Willie Black blurted out with a crooked grin on his face. "We are the circle. When our sponsors retire, we gon' be the ones who take their place. We gon' run the game and you gon' be the lion at the head of the table calling shots because Big the head nigga in charge. He's the one who put all this together, and he chose you to fill his shoes when he retires."

"Big is like a father to me. He's been looking out for me and my homies since we were kids. He said he chose me because he sees something in me."

"Yeah, I know what he see in you. He seesyou ain't no rat and he know you'll leave a man brain on the floor for the right price. That's what he sees," Willie Black said as he puffed deeply on the blunt.

"I'll leave anybody's brain on the floor for nothing if Big told me to. Like I said, he is the closest thing to a father that I got.

"And that's why he chose you. That's why we all got chosen by our sponsors. It's all about love and loyalty, homie. Money over morals and death before disgrace. Our foundation is built on that," Willie Black said, passing Bruno the blunt. "Welcome to the life, homie, ain't no turning back now."

THIRTY-FIVE

The Locos had smoked so many blunts that they couldn't get any higher. Bruno had officially been sponsored by Big, which was a cause for celebration. Their custom painted trucks were the only ones parked in the Peabody parking lot. The Four Locos were posted up on a picnic table, finishing the last swallows of malt liquor inside their Colt 45 bottles. They were drunk, high, and for some reason, Orlando was howling at the full moon shining in the sky.

"Perfect reason they tell you to say no to drugs," Mason joked.

"His true nature coming out, old pitiful dog ass boy," Bruno joined in.

"Y'all ain't gon' use me as yo' entertainment," Orlando slurred. "I'm smashed, but I'm straight enough to knot ya head up, boy."

"All bark, no bite." Poncho chuckled. "Anyway, what's up with some food, man? My stomach is touching my back right now."

"Bruh, it's almost three in the morning," Bruno said, checking his watch. "Ain't nothing open this late."

"You a lie. Waffle House stays open twenty-four hours a day," Poncho corrected.

"Damn. I forgot all about Waffle House. That sounds good right about now. Let's do it."

The Locos staggered back to their whips, hopped in and peeled out. On the way there, Bruno lit up a blunt while Deuce Komradz song, "We Be Riding" flowed through his speakers. His eyelids were heavy from the weed smoke and his thoughts drifted back in time to his first date with Savannah. It was the most fun he'd ever had in his life. It was crazy. After all those years had passed, he was still in love with her. He wondered, after all these years, if they could pick up where they left off. When the Four Locos pulled their trucks into the Waffle House parking lot, they were amazed by how many people were there. Orlando, Mason, and Poncho fired up another blunt outside while Bruno walked inside to get a table. Some guys who recognized him walked over and paid their respects. The restaurant was packed.

THIRTY-SIX

S he never saw it coming. Savannah, Mia and Savannah's boyfriend for the last three years, Stan, were settling into their booth inside the Waffle House on Troy Highway. After a long night of partying and dancing at Club Diamonds, they all agreed on getting something to eat before calling it a night. The restaurant was packed with young people who weren't quite ready to go home yet. The establishment had quickly evolved into one of the hottest after-hour spots on the southside. Savannah really didn't want to be there because it made her think about Bruno. It's where they had their first date. He was the only guy she ever loved. They were supposed to be forever, then whop! She hadn't heard from him ever again. What they shared once upon a time had been a curse and a blessing. She gave her heart to him, and he threw it away, shattering it into a million pieces. She was devastated.

It took her five long years to even entertain the idea of becoming involved in another relationship. That's when she hooked up with Stan. She was in her junior year at Sidney Lanier High School while he was a senior at Faulkner University. They met at the Thanksgiving Day Parade in downtown Montgomery and had been together ever since. Mia couldn't stand him. She thought that he was insecure, controlling, arrogant and carried himself like a real saltine. Savannah agreed that he was kind of uptight. However, she believed that was just the way successful, college educated men acted. He gave her a sense of stability, exactly what she needed in her life. At least he wasn't gay or in prison. Besides, being with somebody was better than being alone. He had his faults, but when it was all said and done, he was there. Normally, he didn't frequent establishments on the urban sides of town, but he'd recently seen the movie "Boyz in the Hood" for the first time and his appetite for hood nigga culture was unexplainable.

"Hey, baby. Look at that freak with all the weave in her hair standing by dude with those gold teeth," he said, laughing. "This is embarrassing."

Mia rolled her eyes. Savannah cleared her throat.

"Yeah, to each his own," Savannah replied. "Let's just mind our own business."

"That's a good idea," Mia seconded. "Or one of those gold teeth wearing dudes might put their foot in your ass."

A lot of dudes inside the Waffle House were staring at Savannah and Mia. They were trying to figure out what those two dime pieces were doing with this lame cat. It was only a matter of time before one of these men vocalized their thoughts. It wouldn't be sweet. In the middle of Savannah cursing herself for agreeing to come here with Stan, she never noticed the cat who just walked in and was watching her intensely.

THIRTY-SEVEN

As Bruno scanned the inside of the Waffle House trying to find an empty booth, he saw her. The girl he thought about every second of every day for the last eight years. She was recklessly beautiful. Her skin complexion, the color of melted butter, highlighted by a pair of eyes which resembled two princess cut diamonds on the sculptured face of an African goddess. She had a radiant smile, and her teeth were like tiny milk white pearl pillows protected by a fresh juicy pair of naturally full pouty lips. All of this accompanied by a bubbly body with the creamy succulent curves of a 1950s pin up girl. She was sexy. She was stunning. She was sweet southern brown sugar at its finest. Savannah Parker was the shit.

She wore a pair of tight black jeans, a white blouse and a black leather jacket. Bruno's mind couldn't comprehend what he was seeing. She had stepped out of his imagination and into his reality. The girl sitting beside her was none other than Mia Monroe. She was knock-you-on- your ass sexy. She had a petite body that looked like it was worked out in a gym religiously.

She wore a tight tan dress that showed off all her assets. She had soft, golden brown skin and hair so black and silky it looked like she was wearing a wig. He couldn't believe how these girls had blossomed into beautiful women. There was a square dude sitting at the table with them. This cat looked like an elementary school teacher or a church choir director or something like that. He seemed harmless. Maybe he was their gay homeboy. Either way, Bruno had to talk to Savannah.

"What can I get y'all to eat?" the waitress asked.

Before Savannah or Mia could respond, Stan began ordering for all of them.

"Yeah. Let us get three waffles with scrambled eggs and hash browns on the side," he said.

"Okay. What about something to drink?" The waitress asked.

"Let me get a glass of milk, orange juice for her and a peach drink for my little peach cobbler."

Bruno walked up and interrupted. "Nah, hood. She likes strawberry," he said with a twinkle of malice in his eyes.

It was so quiet at the table, you could hear a rat piss on cotton. It took a few ticks for Mia to recognize him.

"Oh My God, Bruno!" she screamed, jumping up from the table.

He smiled as she hugged him so tight he thought his neck was going to break.

"I missed you so much," she said, "Look at you."

"Hell naw. Look at you, girl. You look amazing."

Savannah was in shock. All the color had drained from her face. She stared at Bruno, momentarily speechless. He looked completely different since the last time she'd seen him. He was taller, bigger, more muscular and covered in tattoos. He was a man. The type of man who puts fear in lesser men. The kind of man women drooled over and wanted. As he stared at her with those trademark cruel eyes of his, she felt the tiny hairs on the back of her neck stand up. This was her Bruno in the flesh. *No!* She told herself. Her Bruno had disappeared off the face of the earth without a trace eight years ago. Stan was her man now and she had to be woman enough to control this awkward situation.

"What's up, Savannah? You're still the prettiest girl I ever laid eyes on," he said. Savannah blushed hard.

"What's up wit ya, you ain't got nothin' to say to me?" he asked with a smirk on his face. Savannah hadn't realized she was holding her breath until she exhaled. After regaining her composure, she eased up from the seat, and stood face to face with Bruno. Everybody was staring at them inside of the restaurant.

"How long have you been out?"

"A few weeks. I went by your Aunt Pam's crib the other day, but don't nobody stay there anymore."

"She moved a few years ago. She's staying in Red Lion Apartments now." Her silky voice made his heart race.

"I've missed you more than you'll ever know," he said, moving closer into her personal space. Without asking permission, he unbuttoned the top button of her blouse, revealing the diamond necklace he'd given her years ago.

"I knew in my heart you'd still be wearing it."

She chewed on her bottom lip. He tucked a strand of sandy brown hair behind her ear. Then he hugged her as if she belonged to him and kissed her softly on the lips. She tasted like a combination of sweet milk and honey. She put up a token of resistance, but not for long. When the kiss ended, she felt woozy.

"My man is sitting behind us," she whispered.

"Fuck him," Bruno whispered back, then kissed her again.

An uncomfortable silence engulfed them. Stan was

confused and frozen in his seat. Mia was pleasantly shocked. All eyes were on Savannah and Bruno.

"I'm staying at my mama's house in Regency Park until I can get on my feet. You still remember where it is?" he asked. She nodded. "Good. You still my girl, Savannah. I'll still body one over you," he said, glancing at Stan. Savannah didn't respond. Her mouth couldn't form any words. He kissed her softly one last time on the cheek.

"Take it easy, Mia," he said.

"All right, Bruno," she said with a mischievous grin. "We'll see you later."

He turned around and walked towards the door where his homeboys were standing, enjoying the show.

"What it do, Bruno?" Orlando asked.

"Let's get out of here."

"But we just got here, hood. I'm hungry and Savannah and Mia are fine as hell. No disrespect."

"None taken," Bruno replied. "We'll eat somewhere else. Let's go," Bruno said, walking.

His homeboys followed him out of the Waffle House.

When Savannah sat back down at the table, she was still in shock.

"Who the hell were them dudes?" Stan asked angrily.

"The Apocalypse," Mia replied.

"Mia!" Savannah snapped.

"The one who was talking to Savannah rides the white horse, and his name is death."

"Mia, stop it!" Savannah snapped again.

"Ok...Ok... My bad." Mia giggled. "But it's the truth."

To say Stan was mad would've been an extreme understatement. He hadn't said one word to Savannah since they'd dropped Mia off at her apartment. Riding in absolute silence inside of his Nissan 300Zx, Savannah leaned back in the passenger's seat, her thoughts zeroed in on Bruno. She couldn't believe how much he'd changed since the last time she saw him. He wasn't a child anymore and neither was she. Stan was in a pissy mood. She'd figure out a way to make it up to him after he calmed down some.

Damn! Was she tripping? She wondered if Stan's life was in danger. Bruno was definitely capable of killing him in order to get what he wanted. The situation could spin out of control real fast. She would just have to find the time to talk to Bruno one on one. She'd make him understand that she was with Stan now and what they had once upon a time was no more. It was as simple as that. From somewhere in the deepest, darkest corner of her mind, she wondered what it would be like to make love to Bruno. Physically, he was built like an urban gladiator. When he kissed and held her earlier, she felt like he'd cast some kind of spell over her. He could've done whatever he wanted to her, and she wouldn't have had either the power or the will to make him stop. If what happened was so upsetting to Stan then why the hell didn't he say anything to Bruno. It was Bruno who was kissing and rubbing on her, not the other way around. Yeah, it was probably the safe move to keep his mouth shut because Bruno would've smashed him. Still, wasn't he a man just as much as Bruno? Stan just sat there like a punk while Bruno did everything but screw her in front of Mia and everybody inside of the restaurant. What kind of weak ass shit was that? She was beginning to have her doubts about Stan.

Thank God they were pulling into the parking lot of her apartment complex because she felt a serious migraine coming on. Damn! Stan parked and took his key out of the ignition, which meant that he was planning on going upstairs to the apartment with her. She didn't feel like dealing with him anymore that night, but oh well. There was no better time than the present to patch up things between them. She might as well get it over with. She unlocked her front door and walked inside. Stan followed.

"Look, Stan, I know you are upset..."

Before she could finish speaking, he'd smacked her hard in the face. She fell against the wall. Her nose was bleeding, dripping blood into the palm of her hands. She stared at the blood drops in shock. She was confused as to what was happening. Did Stan just hit her? Impossible. He'd never done anything like that before. But there he was, standing in front of her aggressively with a crazed expression on his face.

"I'm your man! Do you hear me!" he yelled. Either you respect me or..."

Before he could finish speaking, Savannah had punched him so hard in the face that it damn near knocked him out. Unable to balance himself on rubbery legs, he fell face first through the living room table. She straddled him on the floor, digging her nails into his face and punching him on the side of his head. She was in a fighter's stance, ready to attack again with tears in her eyes. He stood in front of her trying to catch his breath, obviously not wanting to fight anymore.

"Savannah, I'm sorry. I don't know what got into me," he tried to explain.

"I want you out of my house, Stan. Now!" she shouted.

"Aight, I'll go, but I really am sorry. I'll let you just chill and I'll call you tomorrow." He turned around and walked out the door.

Savannah looked at the blood on her blouse. She ran outside after Stan and saw him about to walk down the two flights of stairs to the parking lot.

"Stan, wait," she said.

He turned around to face her, praying they could go back inside and talk, but that wasn't the case. She punched him square in the face, which sent him crashing violently down the concrete steps. He lay on the ground twisted up and moaning in agony. She stormed back inside of the apartment and slammed the door. Not wanting to break down in tears, she called Mia on the phone. Needless to say, Mia was sitting inside Savannah's apartment fifteen minutes later. There were two things Savannah could always depend on. One was her best friend. The other was her right hook.

THIRTY-EIGHT

I t was a cool, crisp Monday morning. Bruno was sitting on his mother's porch smoking a Newport. He'd made sure that Bella got on the school bus safely and now he was enjoying the fresh morning air. His mother had left for work about thirty minutes ago. So, he pretty much had the crib to himself. He wondered what Savannah was doing. She'd grown up to be painfully beautiful. He couldn't figure out what she saw in that lame cat she claimed was her boyfriend. The two of them just didn't match. Hell, in his mind, she didn't match up well with any man other than himself. Screw it. He'd probably end up having to murk the lame because there was no one on the face of the earth who was going to keep him away from her. When he kissed her that night, she tasted even better than he remembered. A good woman is worth fighting for and in his mind, Savannah was worth killing for. He had to figure out a way to get her back.

A loud car horn pulled him out of his thoughts. When he looked up, he saw Big and Kesha in a black cherry, 1957

Chevrolet Bel Air parked in front of his house. He walked up to the driver's side window.

"What up, y'all? What y'all got goin' on?"

"We supposed to be goin' to pick up some stuff for Big's birthday party this weekend, but he claims he needs to talk to you first," Kesha said, pouting.

"Be patient, baby. Just let me shout at the kid real quick," Big said, giving her a kiss on the cheek.

He got out of the car and walked with Bruno up to the front porch.

"Listen, kid, I got somethin' I need you to handle for me."

"Yeah, Big. Whatever you need, I got you."

"Well, I got some girls that work up and down the Boulevard. That strip is a gold mine. On a good night, I can easily pull in like five grand or better. Anyway, there's a holier than thou guy who owns a gas station that sits directly across the street from the Greyhound bus station. Anytime he sees any of our girls working the scene, he either tries to talk them into leaving the game or he's calling the cops on them. I had to bail six girls out of jail last week. That cost money, which means he's costing me money. Which means he's a problem. I don't want you to murk him, but I do want you to send him a message."

"What's the message?" Bruno asked.

"The message is for him to stay out of my business and off the Goddamn phone with the police."

"How do you want me to do it?"

"Look, kid, your job is to fix problems and show results. You dig what I'm saying. I don't want to hear about the labor pains, just show me the baby."

Bruno laughed. "I'll take care of it, Big."

"And that's why I sponsored you, my boy," Big said, handing him a piece of paper with the guy's name and the directions to his house. "I know you'll handle it. Now, I gotta

get back to Kesha before she blows a fuse. And make sure
you're at my block party this weekend. It's gon' be the whole
thang," Big said, patting Bruno on the shoulder and strolling
back to his car.

Bruno knew Big loved and trusted him. But he also knew
that if he didn't handle his business, it would be his ass.

THIRTY-NINE

2420 Arrowhead Drive

Poncho walked up to the front door carrying an all-purpose bag with his tools inside and pressed the doorbell. An average looking blonde woman in her early forties answered the door.

"Hello, Ma'am, I'm Jose Sanchez. I'm scheduled to do some lawn work for Mr. Malone. Is he home?"

"Yes, he's my husband. We just sat down for supper. Hold on, I'll go get him," she said with a friendly smile.

"No need, ma'am. Why don't we all go get him?" Poncho smiled back.

Bruno, Mason, and Orlando came from out of nowhere and all four men forced their way inside the house. Bruno pointed his Glock at the back of her head, forcing her to lead them to the dining room. The woman was terrified, trembling like a leaf. Somehow, she pulled herself together and did as she was told. When they walked into the dining room, Mr. Malone was sitting at the table, along with his two young sons, eating dinner. Mr. Malone was a short, pudgy, white man with pale skin and receding hairline. Even though he didn't appear to have an aggressive bone in his body, his temper immediately exploded.

"What the hell are you people doing in my house?!"

Mason immediately grabbed his head, shoving it face first inside a large serving bowl of steaming hot mashed potatoes. He screamed like a woman as the hot spuds burned his face.

"Get your boys and go stand over there against the wall," Bruno told Mrs. Malone in a calm voice. She did exactly as she was told. "Now stand there and be very quiet. This will be all over soon." She nodded her head.

After Mason released Mr. Malone's head from the bowl of potatoes, he fell out of the chair onto the floor in agonizing pain.

"Mr. Malone, how you doin' this evening?" Bruno asked with a sympathetic smile.

"There's money in the safe in my bedroom. You can have it. Just take it and go," he begged.

"Well thank you, sir. I'll be glad to take it off your hands when we are done here. But first, we need to talk about your actions at that piece of shit store of yours on the boulevard."

"I... I don't understand what's going on."

"Well, it's been brought to my attention that you on a mission to stop prostitution in the area and you gettin' police involved." Bruno shook his head. "You pissing off a lot of bad people."

"So, that's what this is about?" he asked, his temper quickly beginning to surface again. "You're nothing but a low life pimp making a profit off desperate women and underaged girls. You're a bottom feeder."

Bruno took a slow, deep, calming breath.

"I ain't no pimp. The man I work for could possibly be considered one, but it ain't my style. I specialize in discipline and punishment. Let me show you what I mean." Bruno nodded at Mason and Orlando. "Y'all strip this smart mouth peckerwood down to his skins."

Mason and Orlando tore off all his clothes then slammed him face down on top of the dining room table. Poncho reached inside of his bag and pulled out a thick, industrial extension cord.

"The Good Book says if you spare the rod, you'll spoil the child," Bruno said with a treacherous look in his eyes. "Mrs. Malone, you might want to cover your kids' eyes. It's about to get ugly in here."

She made her children turn and face the wall. Mason and Orlando each secured one of Mr. Malone's arms, holding him in place on the table. Bruno nodded at Poncho who began viciously whooping Mr. Malone's ass with the extension cord. The man screamed so loud that the dead and buried were disturbed from their eternal sleep. Poncho whipped him like an Alabama redneck disciplining a Mississippi slave. His tiny, pale, white ass flinched every time the extension cord connected with his sensitive, flabby cheeks. More screams. His family huddled in fear against the wall as Bruno stood emotionless beside them. Poncho continued to whip him like a madman. Mr. Malone was screaming and crying now. Tears flooded from his eyes uncontrollably. His wife and kids cried along with him as the beating continued. A mist of blood and blisters formed on the surface of his ass. Poncho whipped him and beat him some more. More screaming, more whipping, until finally... "I won't do it no more, mommy!" the man cried out in an abused child-like voice. "I'll be good. I won't tell nobody!" he cried before pissing all over himself and the dining room table.

Shocked by the man's time travel back into his abusive childhood days, Mason and Orlando let him go. Poncho's arm was throbbing like a bitch in heat. Mr. Malone curled up on the table, naked, shivering and crying.

"Mrs. Malone, from here on out, your husband will mind his own business," Bruno informed her. "And he owes me three thousand dollars a month for as long as he owns the store as payment for me not killing him. If he violates the terms of this contract at any time, I will come back to your lovely home, kill him, rape you and stomp your children to death. Do you understand?!"

Afraid and traumatized, she nodded her head in agreement.

"Fellas, if you'll excuse us, me and Mrs. Malone will be right back. We're going to check on this safe in the bedroom," Bruno said.

When they returned, Bruno had twenty thousand dollars in cash in his hands.

"That's about it, let's dip out of here," Bruno said, smiling. "Mr. and Mrs. Malone, our business for today is done. Y'all enjoy your supper and the rest of your evening."

With that, the Four Locos were gone from whence they came.

FORTY

Big's birthday block party in Regency Park was the place to be. The neighborhood was filled with people, young and old, from all over the Southside. It seemed like every house on the block had barbecue grills going in their front yards. The smell of charcoal, lighter fluid, chicken, ribs and burgers lured the entire community out into the streets. A local DJ kept the music playing and the girls dancing all through the night. It was a celebration. Everybody was sipping some kind of alcoholic drink while the weed heads fired up their blunts and shared them with whoever wanted a taste of exotic. For the most part, everybody knew everybody else, and a good time was had by all. Big, Kesha, Larry O, Tuscaloosa Fresh, Trick Shot, Stick Man, Willie Black and Jay Spray relaxed on Big's porch smoking cigars and enjoying the scene. People were constantly stopping by to show respect to the most powerful men in the city and to wish Big a happy birthday. Big enjoyed all the attention he was receiving from the young women who were constantly kissing him on the cheek and waving at him with desire in their eye as they walked in groups past his home.

"I still got it," he said to Kesha, laughing.

She didn't mind because she knew it was his birthday, and she knew that he loved her to death. So, it all was just harmless fun.

"Yes, you do," she said, giggling.

It was a warm summer night. More and more people flowed into the neighborhood as the evening pressed on. While Big joked and laughed with his guests on the porch, Bruno pulled up and parked his truck in front of the house.

"Happy Birthday, old man. I bet you thought I wasn't gon' be here, huh?"

"What's up, youngster. I knew you'd be here. You my right-hand man," Big said as the two men embraced each other.

"I got you a present," Bruno said. "It's from me, Poncho, Mason and Orlando."

He handed him a gift-wrapped box. Inside was a twenty-four-carat gold Movado watch with an inscription on the back that read, *To the Greatest Dad In the World.* Big was touched. He embraced Bruno while forcing himself not to get too emotional.

"Thanks, kid. This is honestly the best gift I've ever been given."

Bruno pulled two pint bottles of Hennessy from his pocket. "You wanna have a drink with me, old man?" Bruno asked.

"You already know the answer to that."

Bruno twisted the cap, broke the seal and handed a bottle to Big before doing the same to his. They tapped their bottles and drank deeply.

"There's nothing like a good cognac to get the blood pumping," Big said.

"And a good cigar to wash it down," Bruno replied.

"You're a quick learner." He laughed, passing Bruno a Cuban.

"So, how old are you anyway?" he asked, lighting his cigar.

"I'm sixty-seven years young and can still slang pipe with the best of them."

"I know that's real." Bruno laughed.

While most of the Commission and their sponsors were talking to some random young women in the front yard, Larry O was on the far end of the porch watching Bruno shoot the shit with Big. In his mind, Big was playing right into his hands by allowing this young psychopath into their inner circle. He knew the time would come when the Commission would be forced to have Bruno put in an early grave which he would happily be willing to do himself sooner than later. He didn't give a damn that Bruno hadn't ever been charged or convicted with the murders of his baby sister and his little homie. Everybody knew the truth. He knew the truth. He had to be patient. There is a time and place for everything. All debts would be paid in full.

Poncho, Mason and Orlando finally showed. Poncho and Mason were drunk as sailors while Orlando had snorted so much cocaine that his nose was red like Rudolph the Reindeer. Larry O believed these young guys were a time bomb waiting to explode. Nothing good could come from being associated with any of them. But fuck it. There was enough room in the cemetery for all of them. The thought made him smile.

FORTY-ONE

"Why do we gotta do this stupid block party, anyway? We need to be gettin' ready for the cooking project we got due on Monday," Mia said while sitting on Savannah's living room couch, flipping through an Ebony Magazine.

"You don't have to go, Mia. Stan just wants me to go with him and hang out with his cousin for a couple of hours, then we're leaving."

"Yeah, right. He just wants to show you off in front of his cousin, so he can act like he that nigga. Besides, he put his hands on you, and it'll be a cold day in hell before I let you go anywhere with that snake by yourself. I should punch him in the face when he gets over here."

"Don't start, Mia. I was wrong to let Bruno kiss me like that in front of him. Any guy would've lost his temper over something like that. And he ain't just beat me up like you think," Savannah said, trying to convince herself as much as Mia.

"He ain't beat you up like I'm thinking? Are you serious? You actually gon' sit here and make excuses for him?" Mia asked in disbelief.

"I ain't making excuses for him. I'm just saying."

"What are you saying?" Mia asked impatiently.

"I'm just saying we have been best friends since forever. And as my best friend, I am asking you to let it go and come keep me company with these lame ass dudes tonight. Can you do that for me?"

"You know I'm on your side, homegirl," Mia said, giving Savannah's hand a gentle squeeze. "But I still think Stan is a punk ass snake."

A car horn blared from downstairs in the parking lot. Savannah peeked through the window blinds and saw Stan's car.

"He's here. Are you ready to go?"

"Yeah, Savannah. I'm ready, but I still think Stan is-"

"I already know. Stan is a punk ass snake," Savannah said, finishing Mia's sentence.

"Yeah, that's what I'm saying."

"Can we go now?"

"Aight, let's go."

Savannah and Mia were the baddest chicks at the block party. Every cat that drove or walked past them said the same thing. "Damn!" Savannah wore a pair of white denim capris, a bright, multi-colored midriff top that tied around her neck, large hoop earrings and a pair of designer flip flop sandals. Mia wore a white summer dress that was seductively short and the breezy swag of a woman who knew she was the shit. Stan acted exactly as Mia said he would. After he introduced the two young women to his cousin, he dismissed them as if hanging out with beautiful females was boring to him. He was a real corn-ball. Savannah and Mia didn't mind because at least now they could hang out and enjoy the party without him. While they were eating barbecue and talking to some people they knew from back in the day, a young girl tapped Savannah on the shoulder.

"Hey. That fine ass guy over there told me to get your attention."

When Savannah turned to look, she saw Bruno at the house across the street, on the front porch with a group of men. He was wearing a white Nike sweatsuit, a huge gold chain with the matching watch and bracelet, a three-finger gold ring on each hand and a pair of new Jordans. He stood there watching her with cool eyes. Savannah froze. She didn't know what to do.

"What's wrong with you?" Mia asked. "It's just Bruno. Your Bruno."

"He is not mine anymore, Mia," she said, irritated.

"Well, he don't know that. Let's just go over and say hi."

Reluctantly, she let Mia lead her across the street. As they walked into the yard and onto the porch, a slow, lazy smile moved over Bruno's face.

"What's up, Mia?"

"Hey, Bruno."

"I still can't believe how sexy you are."

"Thank you, Bruno," she said, blushing.

"And you, Miss Savannah Parker. You'll always and forever be the prettiest girl in the building." He touched his lips to hers. "And that's the truth."

Her knees went weak, and she felt light headed. She thought it was ridiculous how he made her feel so vulnerable just being near him.

"Why don't y'all go talk on the side of the house," Mia suggested. "So that you-know-who don't walk by and get the wrong idea."

"I personally don't care what ideas he gets. But, out of respect for Savannah, I think it's a good idea," Bruno said with a grin on his face.

"After you," Savannah said as she made a face at Mia.

The two of them walked to the side of the house where Bruno leaned against the wall and smiled.

"What are you smiling about?" she asked.

"It just feels good being alone with you."

"Really?"

"Yea, you don't believe me?"

"I believe actions speak louder than words," she said, still feeling some kind of way about him not contacting her for all those years he was gone.

"I feel ya," he said, never breaking eye contact. "So, what you got goin' on in your life?"

Savannah swallowed hard. The sound of his voice was pleasing to all her senses. She felt like she could confess to him every one of her deepest, darkest secrets. He was familiar and forbidden at the same time. He was Bruno Santana, just as she remembered him.

"Are you really interested, or are you just in mack mode?"

"What do you think?" he asked in a smooth, low voice.

He looked at her as if he was looking inside her soul. So deep, she thought he could see everything she was. Her heart trembled.

"Well, I graduated from Lanier two years ago. Me and Mia ended up taking culinary classes at Trenholm Tech. We both got jobs at Pierce Soul Food Restaurant on Fairview. Now we're working in the kitchen. And I got my own place now over in Amesbury Apartments. That's about it, other than the boyfriend thingy."

"Are you serious?" he asked, shaking his head in disbelief.

"What?"

"You graduated high school, you goin' to college, and you got yo' own crib. Baby, I'm so proud of you," he said, hugging her then giving her a gentle kiss. "You doin' it big, baby. You on yo' way to the top. Ladies and gentlemen, the legendary Chef Savannah Parker."

"It ain't all that, but if I keep working hard, one day I might just be somebody," she said, biting her lower lip.

"You always been somebody to me." He softly kissed her lips.

It felt good to once again be the object of Bruno's affection. Almost too good. But it was wrong. She was in a relationship with Stan even if he was a stick in the mud.

"Bruno, stop it," she pleaded, pushing him away. "I got a man, and you have to respect that."

His heart sank. With those words, she'd chosen another man over him. It was an impossible reality to accept. His eyes burned into hers.

"Savannah, I know you got a man. But no, I don't respect it. I just can't."

"That's not fair, Bruno. You had the chance to be with me and you chose not to. So let me move on with my life," she said, feeling emotional.

"Do you know what fair is?" Reaching out, he touched her cheek. "A fair is a place where pigs and cows get blue ribbons. I love you, Savannah, and ain't nothin' you can do 'bout it."

A lump formed in her throat. "I can't." She pushed his hand aside and stormed away.

She didn't understand her feelings, and she didn't know how to deal with them. Bruno acted like they'd been separated for a couple of months instead of eight years. It was confusing and she needed space to think things over clearly. Which is exactly what he wanted. Bruno knew Savannah better than she knew herself. He wanted to overwhelm her with emotions, and when the right moment arrived, he was going in for the kill. Little did he know, the opportunity would be waiting for him in front of Big's crib.

FORTY-TWO

Mia was in the front yard talking to Larry O when Savannah came around from the side of the house. She hadn't expected to run into Larry at the block party and was grateful Savannah gave her an excuse to get away from him. The two of them had a history together and it was obviously over with, but Larry kept popping back up in her life like a bad dream. Savannah seemed upset, so Mia immediately went over to check on her.

"What's wrong?" Mia asked, concerned.

"Talking to Bruno is like talking to a rock. He only sees things his way and it's getting on my nerves. Are you ready to go yet?"

Before Mia could respond, Stan and his cousin were walking in their direction from across the street.

"Woman, are you crazy? What the hell you doing over there with all them broke ass bums?!" he yelled. "You think I'm something to play with? Bring your stupid ass on!" He snatched her arm and yanked her into the street.

Bruno watched the scene take place as he stood beside Big and Kesha. His blood was boiling.

"You're hurting my arm, Stan!" Savannah shouted.

"You better take your hands off of her," Mia said as she blocked his path.

"Mind your business, Mia," Stan warned her as his cousin burst out laughing.

Bruno couldn't take it anymore. It was time to get involved. Big grabbed his arm to stop him.

"Hold on, kid."

Bruno brushed his arm to the side and walked into the middle of the chaos. His Locos followed.

"Oh now, bruh. You dropped somethin'," Bruno said.

When Stan turned around, Bruno punched him hard in the mouth, knocking out his two front teeth, and dropped him on the ground like a defeated prize fighter. Mason, Poncho, and Orlando took turns brutally stomping his head and body on the concrete. There was a huge crowd standing around cheering and watching the drama unfold.

"Don't do this, Bruno," Savannah pleaded.

Mia grabbed her hand and pulled her out of harm's way. The violent assault continued in the middle of the street. Stan couldn't fight back. He took shot after shot like a human punching bag. His cousin had long since disappeared. He wanted no problems with the Locos.

"Y'all chill out," Bruno ordered the Locos. "Put the bitch on his knees."

The Locos carried out Bruno's order, placing Stan on his knees. His swollen head was the size of a pumpkin.

"Oh now, Swamp Man!" Bruno shouted. "Come here, hood!"

Swamp Man stepped out of the crowd and walked up to Bruno. He was a six-foot-six, three-hundred-pound, dark skinned cat with a bald head and a mouth full of gold teeth. He served time with the Four Locos in prison and had a reputation for extreme violence.

"What's up, hood?" Swamp man asked as he dapped Bruno.

"Who hood this is?" Bruno asked him.

"This our hood," Swamp Man responded.

"That's what I thought, hood."

"This is bad," Savannah said to Mia.

Mia looked at her best friend and could see the fear straining her hazel eyes. Bruno pulled out his Glock and pointed it at Stan's head.

"Hey, schoolboy, you wanna die?" Bruno asked.

"No. No... Please don't kill me!" Stan cried with blood-stained tears streaming down his busted face.

"Are you crying' boy? Men don't cry, bitches do," Bruno said, performing for the crowd. "Now, Swamp Man, show this boy what bitches like."

"Aight, hood," Swamp Man said, laughing.

Swamp Man unzipped his jeans and whipped out his swollen, twelve-inch, purple cock. He held it about four inches away from the tip of Stan's nose.

"Put it in ya mouth, and I won't kill you," Bruno promised him.

Stan was now crying hysterically. He looked in Bruno's eyes and saw nothing but absolute evil. Terror shot through his body like a bolt of lightning. This was a homosexual act, but that never happened to Trey or Ricky in the movie *Boyz In the Hood*. He didn't remember either one of them being forced to suck a cock. What the hell was going on? This was not the time to pretend to be a gangster. There was no doubt that if he didn't do what he was told, he was going to die.

"What's wrong, schoolboy? You look sick. Go ahead and eat it. It'll make you feel better," Bruno said like he was talking to a small child with a tummy ache.

Stan closed his eyes tight and opened his mouth up, his lips trembling like a goldfish. He leaned forward and right before his mouth made contact with Swamp Man's cock, Bruno slammed his foot into the side of his head.

"What the hell's wrong with you, schoolboy? Ain't no fuck niggaz in Regency Park."

The crowd went crazy, throwing four fingers up in the air and cheering like they were at a college football game. They couldn't believe what they witnessed. It was a scene they would tell their children and grandchildren about for years to come. As Stan tried to pull himself up off the ground, beaten, degraded and humiliated, Bruno kicked him hard in the ass.

"Get yo' punk ass out my hood and stay away from my girl."

People were laughing and showing love to the Locos. The demonstration had been laid down to perfection. Not only had everybody been well entertained, but they were also afraid. Nobody wanted to be on the bad side of Bruno and the Four Locos. Big smiled at Bruno, nodding his head in approval at the way Bruno had enhanced the Locos' reputation.

Bruno looked and saw Savannah at the top of the street. She looked at him in disappointment and disappeared into the night.

"Damn!" Bruno said in frustration. "Damn! Damn! Damn!"

FORTY-THREE

A lot of crazy shit had occurred the night before in Regency Park. However, at the moment, none of that mattered. Savannah and Mia were doing what they did best, cooking. The outside world didn't exist when they were putting in work inside of a kitchen. The only thing that mattered was the food. They worked in unison like a fine-tuned machine preparing the project for their afternoon baking class the following day. They were working on a five-layer, white chocolate covered, strawberry, Philadelphia cream cheesecake made from scratch. It was an ambitious recipe they'd created together to cement their status as the wonder women of their culinary arts class. They worked with efficient precision and on instincts without conversation for five straight hours. The only sounds in Savannah's kitchen were the soulful sounds of Kenny G playing his saxophone through the CD player on the kitchen table. Their culinary skills were flawless, and they were in the zone. After the cake was finished, and Savannah had generously spread the homemade cream cheese icing over every square inch of cake, the young women sat down at the kitchen table and relaxed.

"What do you think about the cake?" Savannah asked as she licked a dab of frosting from her index finger.

"It's gonna blow Chef Alexander's mind," Mia replied.

"You think? I just hope it's good enough to get us in his apprenticeship kitchen next summer."

"Be for real, Savannah. When have we ever cooked anything that was second best to anybody?" Mia asked with an insulted expression.

"Well, at least one of us is confident."

"Yeah, and you should be too. The proof is in the product," Mia declared with pride.

Savannah took a delicate bite of a leftover, white chocolate covered strawberry.

"You ain't lying, gurl. These are the bomb," Savannah joked, rolling her neck and using her best hoodrat voice.

"Ain't no question about it," Mia responded, taking a sip from her bottle of Perrier water. "But I do wanna ask you something now that we're finished with the cake."

Savannah arched a skeptical eyebrow.

"Where do things stand between you and Stan?"

Savannah knew this question was coming sooner or later, so she wasn't surprised by it. She popped the rest of the strawberry in her mouth.

"I don't know, Mia. I called this morning to check on him. He said he'd be aight then he hung up in my face."

"What? That ain't right, girl. You ain't did anything to him."

"I know right. I tried to call him back like four or five times and he wouldn't even answer the phone."

"Nooo, girl. That's some real bull right there," Mia said, trying not to crack up. "I still can't believe he was about to give that big black dude some head."

She could hardly get it out from her and Savannah laughing so hard. Tears were coming from their eyes. Mia's stomach was hurting. It was a laugh fest. Savannah was carrying on so bad, she almost wet herself. Somehow, Stan's traumatic experience turned into their entertainment for the evening. This thought caused Savannah to feel guilty. Suddenly, her perception changed. Things inside of her apartment that she associated with Stan seemed weird. She noticed the bodybuilding magazine he'd left on the counter. There was a huge, oiled up black man on the cover wearing a bikini bottom. It never bothered her before, but now it all seemed suspect as hell. She then looked at the framed picture of Stan on the living room table. In the picture, he was on the dance floor at some club doing a funny dance to some random rock-n-roll song. She used to think he looked cute in the picture, but now it seemed that the man in the photograph was obviously a homosexual. She couldn't believe it. Bruno had fucked up how she looked at Stan. Mia noticed Savannah wasn't laughing anymore and quickly pulled herself together.

"Hey, I'm sorry. I wasn't trying to make fun of the situation," Mia said, attempting to be serious. "I was just trying to cheer you up."

Savannah had gone from solemn to tickled, then to sad and now mad as hell.

"This is all Bruno's fault! He ruined everything!" she shouted then stormed off to her bedroom, slamming the door behind her.

Mia took another sip from her bottled water.

"Stan the ghetto gagger," she said, killing herself laughing. "Help me Lawd Jesus."

FORTY-FOUR

"I'm telling you, Big, I have a three hundred and thirty pound monkey on my back," Trick Shot said as he and Big conversed over breakfast and coffee inside of Willie's Diner. "I can't sleep. I can't eat. I can't even screw my wife, the poor thing. I'm losing my mind, and I don't know who else to turn to."

"Seriously? By the size of your gut and that plate sitting in front of you, it don't look like you missin' too many meals to me," Big said jokingly.

"Come on, Big, I'm serious here. I got problems on top of problems. I need some assistance."

"A wise man once said that problems are actually opportunities because they give you the chance to succeed by solving your own problems."

"Really? Well, I got so many opportunities, it's becoming a goddamn problem," Trick Shot replied dryly.

Big laughed hard. "Aight, aight. Tell me what you got goin' on?"

"Thank you. It's a group of dread head dudes outta Mobile.

They opened up shop on Alexander Street. They're pushing everything from weight to grams. The quality ain't as good as ours, but the weight is cheaper, and their bags are almost three times bigger than ours. I'm losing money on both ends of the scale. That means you're losing money too."

"You did say Alexander Street, right?"

"Yeah, Big, Alexander Street."

Big leaned his elbows on the table and sipped his coffee. "The last time I checked, Alexander Street was on the west-side. Get your soldiers to take care of it."

"You think I ain't tried that? Jay Spray sent four of our people in to handle it. They caught 'em up at Club Unique and got into a shootout. Three of our people got shot. One is in critical condition. The dreads came out of it without a scratch and they're still pumping the block."

"How many dread heads are there?"

"It's six of 'em and a girl."

Big was appalled. "You gon' sit here and tell me six hard legs and a broad done took over one of yo' blocks and ain't nothin' you can do 'bout it?" Big said in a low voice with a look of disgust on his face.

"I know, it's an embarrassment to my whole crew, but we ain't built for urban warfare. We stack paper. These dudes are on another level. They smoked four of my best men. This shit is getting ugly. I need to have it taken care of before the streets get to talkin', or even worse, the rest of the Commission finds out." Trick Shot wiped a stream of sweat from his forehead. "That kid of yours and his crew match up better with these kinds of people. We go back a long way. So, you know I wouldn't come to you if I didn't have to."

"Trick, you're one of my oldest and closest friends. But this situation you in ain't good. If Larry O or Tuscaloosa Fresh find out, they gon' wanna cross you out and split up the westside between themselves."

"I understand, Big. That's why I'm ready to pay you a hundred and fifty grand to take care of it for me and keep it on the hush."

Big picked up his coffee cup and took a sip, looking at Trick Shot over the rim.

"If you were anybody else, I'd take over the westside myself. But you're my friend and we're in this life together. So, I'll see that it's taken care of and kept quiet. But make sure you have that hundred and fifty stacks. I'm gon' let my boys split it up so they can start off in this life the right way."

"Thank you Big," Trick Shot said, relieved. "Thank God for your mother and father. I owe you big time."

"You have no idea," Big said. "Now finish your breakfast. It's gettin' cold."

Big drained his coffee cup, rose from the table and exited the diner.

FORTY-FIVE

Club Main Event was filled to capacity. It seemed like everybody in the city was in attendance. Tela's song, "You Can't Tell" had the entire club singing along with its hardcore lyrics. The Four Locos were dressed in Polo Jeans, basketball jerseys and Timberland boots. Their necks and wrists were draped in jewelry. This was their first time inside of a night club and they were enjoying themselves to the fullest. All the homies from back in the day and men they'd served time with in prison were showing them love and paying for their drinks. Females were showering them with hugs and kisses while dudes who'd only heard of their reputation stared in awe. The scene was surreal. Mason and Poncho were on the dance floor doing their thing with a group of college girls while Orlando made up for lost time with an old fling, Samille.

Unlike Bruno, Orlando kept in touch with Samille throughout his entire eight-year prison bid. This broad was a sight for sore eyes. She wore a micro mini skirt, low cut tank top and spike heels. Time had truly been good to Samille. She had luscious dark skin, a pretty face and body that would make a man's jaw drop through the floor. She and Orlando had been tossing back shots of Tequila since they'd entered the club, so all of their inhibitions were gone with the wind. Orlando's hands roamed freely and thoroughly over every square inch of her beautiful body. It had got to the point where the club security threatened to kick them out if they didn't turn down the heat a couple of notches. It was a small thing to a giant, so Orlando acknowledged but continued with his hands-on examination.

Bruno observed Orlando and the rest of the club crowd from the shadows. He sipped on a rum and coke while thinking about the only woman he'd ever been in love with. He wondered where she was and who she was with. She couldn't possibly be laid up with that Stan guy. Not after the way he humiliated him in front of her at Big's block party. It had been a classic Loco moment and he didn't regret any of it. Why should he? In his mind, Savannah would always belong to him. In between the sips of rum, Bruno was snatched aggressively from his thoughts when he observed Savannah enter the club. She was with Mia.

As they walked towards the bar, they attracted stares from men like flies to shit. Savannah wore a light brown miniskirt with a matching see-thru blouse and high heels with her pedicured toes exposed. Mia wore an off-the-shoulder sweater, short tight skirt and designer sandals. Bruno watched the two young women purchase a couple of mixed drinks from the bar then make their way over to a small table where they sat down. A few minutes later, two older men joined their table. They talked for a while to the gorgeous young women then signaled for the waitress to bring over a bottle of champagne. The women allowed these men to sit down and the macking ritual was officially in session. Bruno told himself that a true player would respect the game and let the pieces fall where they may, but Bruno was no mutherfucking player. He was a gangster and

Savannah was off limits. Fighting to maintain his temper, he walked up to the cozy group and interrupted their chit chat.

"What's up, ladies, long time no see," Bruno said, his dark eyes warning immediate danger. Savannah picked up on the vibe instantly, but Mia was clueless.

"Hey, Bruno. Is this club live or what?" Mia said, smiling.

"Yeah, it's something. Especially now that you and Savannah are here."

"Thanks. This is Fred and Vince. They're visiting from Birmingham for the weekend. We were just telling them some places they should check out while they're down here," Savannah said as a feeling of dread swept over her.

Fred stood and extended his hand, but Bruno just stared at him with cold, accusing eyes.

"I don't shake hands with dead men. I only pour out liquor for 'em," Bruno said, taking a sip of his rum and spitting it on Fred's shoes.

"I feel ya, Frat. Maybe me and Vince should be leaving. I thank you ladies for your hospitality. Y'all have a good evening."

"You too," the women said in awkward unison.

As the men turned and walked away, Bruno called out to them.

"Hey, homie, don't forget yo' liquor," he said, tossing them the open bottle of champagne that spilled all over Vince when he caught it.

Bruno sat down across from Savannah.

"Why you ain't come by the crib or call me? You got me waitin' by the phone like a sucker."

"You're a real jerk, Bruno. Those guys you just disrespected didn't do anything to be treated like that. What the hell is your problem?" Savannah was furious. Her hazel eyes flared as she swept a sandy brown strand of hair back with her manicured fingernails.

"Why you standin' up for them clowns? All they wanted to do was fuck. You don't even know them. Fuck 'em."

Savannah leaned across the table, staring directly into his eyes.

"You're out of your fuckin' mind. You can't treat people like that. People you don't even know. And just so you know, what you did to my boyfriend was horrible. What type of sick person would even think to do some sick ass shit like that?! You're no different than how Alfonso used to be. I don't even know you anymore!"

Savannah was enraged. She looked at Bruno in pure disgust. He opened his mouth to speak, but she stuck her hand out.

"Don't say another word to me."

"Savannah, I was just-" he started to say.

"Don't try to explain!" she snapped. "I'm so pissed off at you right now, I don't even want to look at you!"

With that said, the two women stood up from their seats and left.

Bruno slammed his fist on the table in frustration. "Fuck!"

FORTY-SIX

Bruno had been in a dark mood ever since Savannah left the club. The excitement of being there for the first time diminished. The electricity had been sucked from the atmosphere. His view of the club scene changed drastically. The scene was like Dodge City with its outlaw population. Hustlers, hoes, gangbangers, thugs, and conmen infested the crowd. He drowned his frustrations in rum and whisky shots. The more he drank, the less human the club crowd seemed to him. Instead of attractive women, he saw leeches in miniskirts, pushup bras, and excessive makeup. They lounged around the bar while poisonous snakes wearing baseball caps and designer jeans rolled lies and fake promises from their serpent tongues into the ears of drunken whores who had nothing going on upstairs to think with. He fantasized about pulling out his Glock and shooting up the place, mercifully putting them out of their misery. He couldn't stomach anymore. It was time to get the hell out of Dodge.

Meanwhile, Samille was having a good time on the dance floor. Maybe too good of a time if you asked Orlando. She was nasty dancing with two thirsty men,under the strobe light. A tramp in heat. Their bodies were talking a foreign language, which everyone who witnessed it clearly understood as pure, unadulterated, carnal lust. Rhythmic porn intended for mature audiences only. A sexual teasing that was so graphic, it was not lady like, even by a slut's standard. Orlando could not take it any longer. Drunk and geeked up on cocaine, he staggered through the crowd, barely able to suppress his rage. He snatched Samille by the arm, dragging her off the dance floor like a rag doll and into the dark shadows of the club.

"What did I do?" she asked with a look of confusion on her face Orlando considered faker than a whore's love.

He slapped the unholy shit out of her again and again. She dropped to the floor like a bag of wet laundry.

"I'm sorry, Orlando!" she cried out.

Hearing her call his name brought him back from the darkness. He pulled her up off the floor. She was sobbing uncontrollably.

"I'm sorry, Orlando. Please don't beat me no more," she begged with tears flooding her eyes.

He gripped her arm tightly. "Relax, don't make a scene."

As hard as she tried, she couldn't stop the tears from falling. She'd never been hit by a man before.

"Stop crying, baby. You know I'm sorry, but I just can't share you with nobody. You mean too much to me."

"You mean a lot to me too, Daddy. I'm sorry," she said softly, wiping away tears.

He slipped an arm around her shoulder and drew her closer to him, kissing her forehead. Healing her pain with his touch as if he were her higher power even though he was no God, and she was no angel. A group of people were watching this troubling scene play out before their eyes with horror and shock written all over their faces. It was time to get the hell out of Dodge.

Over on the dance floor, Poncho was dancing with a redbone chick with big, busty breasts and a bubblicious booty. However, his mind was on the white girl who'd accidentally spilled her drink on him while trying to move through the crowded club. She apologized and offered to pay for his clothes to be cleaned, but he told her not to worry about it. Accidents happen. This girl was Arizona Desert hot with creamy white skin, long, straight, chestnut brown hair, a small, slender body and just enough booty to grab a man's attention. She wore a silk tank top, a tight black leather miniskirt with seamed black stockings and stiletto heels. She was the type of female who ordinary women hated. The only thing more impressive than her looks were her eyes. They were ocean water blue and lethal as boric acid. When the current song ended, Poncho told the redbone chick he'd holler at her later and immediately scanned the club in search of the white girl. Finally, he spotted her standing by the bar, sipping on a drink. He took a deep breath and walked over to the bar.

"Let me get a goose on the rocks with a splash and whatever this sexy woman here is drinking," he told the bartender.

"I'll have a Long Island Iced Tea, and thanks for the drink," she said, smiling.

"Are you gon' tell me your name, or do I have to wait till our second date?" Poncho asked after the bartender delivered their drinks.

She laughed softly. "I'm Shaelyn," she said, offering her hand.

"Shaelyn, that's a pretty name. I'm Poncho," he said, shaking her hand.

"I know who you are," she replied.

"How you know me?"

"Everyone knows who you and your friends are."

"Is that a fact?"

"I'm afraid so, Mr. Poncho."

"What neighborhood are you from?"

"I grew up in the Vineyard," she said with pride.

Poncho was pleasantly surprised. The Vineyard was a rough area where only the treacherous survived.

"So, you're a Southside chick," he said with a smile. "I ain't know white people lived in the Vineyard."

"Me and my mom were the only white folks there. So, yeah, I'm Southside from the womb to the tomb."

Poncho threw up both of his hands, laughing.

"I hear ya. I don't want any problems," he joked.

"You never know, my problems might be your pleasure." She gave him a suggestive smile.

"Really?" he asked with a goofy smile.

"Uh-huh," she said, licking her lips.

"What kind of problems you got, girl? I'm curious."

"I got a serious addiction."

"To what?"

"You'll have to figure it out on your own," she said with a seductive grin.

"You're a handful," he said, laughing. He gulped half of his drink.

"Yeah, that's what I have been told," she replied.

"Seriously though, what's your story?" he asked, lighting a cigarette.

"I don't know. Same old song, just a different singer. Mom has me. Dad leaves me. Mom marries black stepdad. Stepdad moves to the vineyard. Stepdad gets killed and that's the end of that. But that's life, ya know. Rarely does it have a happy ending."

Poncho inhaled a puff of cigarette smoke and exhaled it through his nose.

"I believe folks make their own endings. It's what you make it."

Shaelyn shrugged her shoulders and smiled.

Just then, Mason, Orlando, and Samille strolled up to the bar, slamming the brakes on Poncho's conversation.

"What up, hood?" Orlando said. "This club ain't talkin' 'bout nothin'. We outta here. Bruno's outside in the parking lot, he ready to go."

"Aight, hood. I'm 'bout to bounce too. I'll catch up wit y'all fools on the rebound," Poncho said.

They all dapped each other up then left Poncho and Shaelyn at the bar.

"So, you gon' call me or something?" Shaelyn asked.

"That's cool, but I was hoping we could go to your crib and get to know each other better."

"I thought you'd never ask." She smiled.

It was past time to get the hell out of Dodge.

FORTY-SEVEN

Samille wasn't green by any stretch of the imagination. She knew Orlando was an aggressive man, and when he was geeked up on cocaine, he could be downright abusive. She also knew he was a complicated man and when he wanted to, he could make all her pain melt away like the wax on a lit candle. More importantly, she knew Orlando was a hustler. She believed with all her heart that he was on his way to the top. He was going to be the man someday. And once he arrived, she wanted to be right there by his side. So, after looking herself over in their motel bathroom mirror, she allowed her senses to be open towards his playerish persuasion.

All the remaining resentment she held onto was washed away when he took her in his arms. He kissed her softly as his hand brushed over her hair. She wrapped her arm around his neck while standing on the tips of her toes, so that her lusciously thick body leaned on his. He moved his hands over her body, healing where it ached and yearned. The taste of his tongue in her mouth sent electrical shocks spiraling through her entire system. All her insecurities and stress evaporated because she felt wanted. His eyes told her everything she wanted to hear. That she was the only woman for him and that she was beautiful. When they undressed each other, they admired each other's bodies. He touched her with desperate need, filling her with so much emotion, that when he scooped her up in his arms, she was shivering. He laid her on the bed, then crawled into it with her. The anticipation burning inside her soul made her shout out his name. His hands were rough and violent. A killer's hands. She tensed up under them, arched and whined. She stroked her hand along his manhood. He felt like an African warrior back home from war. A Mandingo warrior. She rolled him over on the bed and licked every inch of his body. Something those stuck-up Southside broads would never do. His moaning was music to her ears. He grabbed and yanked her hair as she orally pleased his pipe like it was the last one left on earth. When she straddled him, she looked down at his guilty face, saw the arrogance in his eyes and smiled. She took him into her, deep and hard and thought to herself that nothing in this wicked world felt better than a gangster's cock.

Meanwhile, on the other side of Cupid's arrow, Poncho didn't know why, but for some reason he was feeling this girl. He'd never messed around with a white girl before and, in fact, he'd never even known one personally. He assumed they were all overly sensitive airheads. However, Shaelyn didn't fit that category. He could relate to her on different levels. The main level was one with her being the lone member of a race raised in an all-black community. Coming up under those circumstances, a person had to have tough skin. Because, even though black is beautiful, niggas is crazy. The black kids terrorized Poncho in elementary school and if it wasn't for the Locos, he probably wouldn't have made it.

Shaelyn kicked off her stiletto heels and lit up a blunt of fruity Poncho had sitting in the ashtray. The windows were rolled down inside the truck, allowing the wind to blow through her hair like one of those sexy snow bunnies in rock n' roll videos. This girl was the real deal. She wasn't some blue blood broad with a lily-white reputation. She was the way, the truth and the light. And the only way to get into heaven was between those long, silky legs. Poncho was quickly becoming a devout follower. Her sparkling blue eyes overwhelmed him. Butterflies fluttered in his stomach, causing him to feel like a teenage boy hooking up with his girlfriend for the first time. As he parked his truck in the parking lot of her apartment complex, he knew this was going to be a night to remember.

"So, what's up?" he asked, lost in her baby blue eyes.

"What you want to be up to?" she responded, eyes twinkling.

She exited the truck, her miniskirt hiking to the top of her thighs. He admired her as she strolled along the walkway leading to her apartment. Her slender hips swayed seductively in her skintight leather skirt. At that point, he never wanted to be with any woman more than he wanted to be with Shaelyn. She unlocked her apartment door. As soon as they were inside, they immediately started kissing sloppily, exploring each other thoroughly and tearing off each other's clothes like a couple of horny teenagers. When they were stripped down to their birthday suits, Poncho picked her up, and carried her into the bedroom. After tossing the bedspread on the floor, they went at each other all night, experiencing pleasures neither of them had ever felt before. It was amazing.

When the early morning sunlight seeped through the curtains, Poncho was drained and completely sprung on this girl. He eased out of bed, started coffee in the kitchen and returned moments later to surprise her with breakfast in bed. Her face lit up.

"Really?"

"I know how to treat a woman. Especially my woman."

"Oh, so I'm your woman now?" she asked with a smile.

"I want you to be."

"Well, we'll see. Maybe if you're lucky, who knows."

He scooped her up playfully in his arms and covered her face with kisses. They made love again and again. Poncho was officially smitten.

FORTY-EIGHT

Sometime during the first murky light of dawn, Savannah drifted off to a restless sleep. She tossed and turned. Turned and tossed. Bruno consumed her thoughts. He'd completely taken over her subconscious. She obsessed over things like, what he was doing when she was at school, when she was alone in her apartment after school and when she woke up frustrated in the middle of the night. When they were kids, he'd killed people as if it were as easy as playing a video game. He was the devil's black sheep. He was dangerous, and apparently, as an adult he was still the same, probably even worse. It would be best to cut all ties with him and leave him in her past where he belonged. She needed to close the chapter to that part of her life. What she really needed was an honest, hardworking man. A man like Stan. Except, she knew that Stan could never look her in the eye again. Not after he'd almost performed oral sex on another man in public to protect himself. Poor Stan. She giggled, but felt horrible after she did it. There was nothing funny about that situation. Bruno had only recently come home and already, his dark side was rubbing off on her. A couple of hours later she stretched in bed as she watched the sunlight pour into her window. She was tired, frustrated and in a shitty mood. Bruno, with his selfish assumptions of them being together, was ruining her life. She had to stop him. Nobody owned her And if that's what he thought, well, screw him, he could think again. She had to nip this shit in the bud. She headed to the bathroom. Bruno had said that he was staying at his mom's crib in Regency Park. That's where she would confront him. She was twenty years old. A grown woman handles small problems before they become large ones. She turned on the water, waited a couple of ticks for it to heat, then stepped under the shower head As the warm water rained down on her, she decided that there was no way around it. Bruno was a loose end and loose ends needed to be cut. She was on her way to becoming a gourmet chef and a business woman. Bruno was a gangster. She dressed in orange capris with a sleeveless white shirt and sandals. She put on some lip gloss, pulled her hair into a ponytail and left. It was slap-ya-mama hot outside. The city had been in the throes of a record heat wave. The inside of her Honda felt like a hot box as she put the key into the ignition. She turned the key, nothing. She turned it over and over again, but still nothing. She slammed her fist on the dashboard and cursed. Her car was a piece of junk. Not only was it an eye sore, it couldn't even be depended on to get her from point A to B. She got out of the car and pitched a fit. She assaulted her Honda with her purse while verbally abusing it. A beautiful red and black old school Ford pickup truck, pulled up in front of her car. She didn't recognize the driver until he rolled down his dark tinted window. Mason Monroe in the flesh, million dollar smile and all.

"What's the problem, Lil Mama?"

"Hey Mason, what are you doing here?"

"I was just driving by and saw you over here going one on one with your car and I was wondering who won."

"It's a piece of crap! But it is all I got until I can save up enough money for another one."

"I feel you. You want me to drop you somewhere?"

"I was on my way to Bruno's house to let him know how much of an asshole he's been lately."

"Whoa!" Mason said, holding up his hands. "I don't want nothing to do with that." He chuckled.

"Well, I guess it's nothing you can do then, Mason," she said, irritated.

Mason studied her for a moment.

"How about I wait here, and you can use my truck to go see him?"

Savannah was delighted.

"Are you serious? I mean, here's the keys to my apartment. You can chill in there and eat whatever you want. I won't be gone long."

"Ain't no rush."

As soon as Mason stepped out of the truck, Savannah gave him a big hug then jumped in and took off. Mason knew Bruno would've wanted him to let her use the truck. Those two were made for each other. He only hoped that they'd hurry up and get past all the drama before it was too late.

FORTY-NINE

"Hello," she said, holding the phone to her ear.

"What up, my little flower?"

"What do you want, Larry?" she said coldly.

"I've been thinking about you and missing you like crazy."

"Really? Have you asked for a divorce yet?"

Mia was in the middle of some bullshit. The older cat she'd been sleeping with on and off for the last sixteen months still hadn't left his nagging wife like he'd promised.

"Damn, Mia! Can't we have a civil conversation without all the drama?"

"Nah, not until you serve your wife with those divorce papers," she said before hanging up the phone in his face.

Larry O was beginning to get on her damn nerves. Always wanting something from her, but never giving anything back in return. Savannah warned her about getting involved with a married man, but she didn't listen to her advice. He'd promised her that he would leave his wife. He swore that the two of them would be together, eventually starting a family of their own. She fell for all of his empty promises, hook, line, sinker. However, the truth had come to light and she saw him for what he truly was. A compulsive liar. No time or use for crying over spilled milk. So she let him go. Praying that he and his wife would live happily ever after. They deserved each other. Anyway, she had plans for the morning with Savannah. It was time to get going. She took a quick satisfying shower and got dressed. She wore a white cropped top, beige tight pants, and a pair of low top Nike running shoes. She grabbed her keys off the kitchen table and left. It was oppressively hot outside. She quickly got inside of her Toyota, started the engine, and crunk up the air conditioner. She checked her hair in the rearview mirror, then made her way over to Savannah crib. After a short drive, she parked beside Savannah' Honda and strolled up the stairs to her apartment. Using the spare key that Savannah gave her, she unlocked the door and walked inside. She was surprised to find Mason sitting on the couch with a huge bowl of cornflakes watching the Smurfs on tv.

"Uhh, hey, Mason," she said. "What are you doing here?"

"Hey, Mia. I'm just waiting on Savannah to get back. I let her borrow my truck to go see Bruno because her car broke down."

"That was nice of you," she said while admiring his profile. He was tall with a lean wiry build, broad shoulders, and dark sleepy bedroom eyes. When he smiled there was no resisting him. Good Lord, he was handsome, she thought to herself.

"I try to be," he responded.

"Huh?" She was embarrassed, hoping she hadn't been thinking out loud.

"Nice. You said that I was being nice, right?"

"Oh, yeah." She smiled nervously.

"Why don't you sit down and eat breakfast with me? It's enough for both of us," he said.

Mia sat beside him on the couch, and before she could

refuse, he was already offering her a spoonful of his cornflakes and milk.

"Go ahead, I promise I ain't got cooties," he joked.

She smiled and accepted it.

"So, what are you doing up so early on a Saturday morning?" he asked.

"Me and Savannah usually go out to breakfast every Saturday morning, and I- I like getting up early anyway."

"Yeah, well I guess it's just me and you this morning," he said, smiling at her.

Mia's heart fluttered. "I guess so."

Even though the central air had the inside of the apartment cool, Mia's palms were sweating.

"Do you ever think about moving away from Montgomery?" she asked after a brief silence.

"Sometimes, I do. When everything seems messed up. But this is my home. Where all of my friends and family are. So, nah, I don't want to leave."

She looked deep into his eyes. "Me either," she replied.

Mason felt a shiver flow through his body. He couldn't be sure, but he felt like Mia was flirting with him. Of course, he found her attractive, extremely attractive. However, he figured she was out of his league. Her caramel brown skin and cat-like eyes made him feel like a clumsy ox and for the first time in a long time, he was at a loss for words.

"I remember when we were in school, I gave Poncho a letter to give to you, but you never responded. It took me a week to write that letter and it was like you blew me off," she said.

"Yeah... I was getting so many letters from girls back then, I guess I didn't notice yours." Mason regretted what he said immediately. He could tell by the expression on her face that he offended her. He felt genuine remorse.

"Hey, Mia, I didn't mean it like that. I just..."

"You don't have to explain, really. It was a long time ago."

"Nah, I wasn't trying to hurt your feelings. It's just that you were always the prettiest girl in school, and I guess I was just intimidated by you. And yeah, I remember getting your letter and the poem you wrote at the end. I read it like a thousand times," he said, laughing. "I wanted to write you one back. But it was like, I just couldn't find the right words to say. I guess I just thought that girls like you were supposed to be with boys like Poncho or Orlando. Me, I was a nobody."

"That's so sweet, Mason, but you were never a nobody to me."

He thought for a moment. "If I knew back then what I know now, we could've had something, huh?"

"Do you still think I'm the prettiest girl?" she asked.

"You are the prettiest girl I know," he said.

Mia blushed. "Yeah, well you've been in prison for the last eight years, so you probably don't know too many girls." She laughed.

Mason smiled. "I wonder if your mouth tastes as good as it looks," he said.

Mia's heart was pounding furiously against her rib. Anticipation flowed through her like a raging river. She dropped her eyes to his mouth and felt an insatiable hunger. Desire flared as Mason leaned in and their lips locked. Her tongue forbiddingly danced with his. Her emotions began to spin out of control. The reckless desire and need made her dizzy. Desperately needing to pull herself together, she placed her hands on his chest and weakly pushed him away. For what seemed like an eternity, the two of them stared into each other's eyes, lost in the maze of attraction.

"I should go," she said, slowly pulling herself up from the couch and heading towards the door. As she reached for the doorknob, Mason called out to her.

"Mia." She turned around, afraid to look into his eyes. "I

was just wondering if later on tonight you wanted to grab a pizza and see a movie or something?"

She digested what he said and smiled. The anxiety quickly evaporated from her eyes. "That sounds nice." She wrote her phone number down on the palm of his hand and kissed him on the cheek. "Make sure you call me, Mason Monroe," she said.

The way his name rolled off of her tongue was like the sweetest music he'd ever heard.

"I'll see you soon, Mia Monroe," he replied.

She smiled and walked out the door. He knew at that very moment she was the one.

FIFTY

S he couldn't have come at a worse time. Savannah was standing on Bruno's front porch, knocking on the door, while he was inside the crib with Erica. Erica promised him that she would teach him a lesson on the birds and bees that he would never forget. She was from around the way and the perfect get-over-my-ex present that a cat could receive. She was a sexy little package, who was young, dumb and eager to please. She was a gift from the thug life Gods. Although, at this moment in time, she was Bruno's worst nightmare. If Savannah thought that he was a piece of shit before, she would definitely flush his hopes and dreams of them being together down the toilet after seeing Erica. But what choice did he have? He had to answer the door. With that said, he pulled himself together and opened the front door.

"What's up, Savannah?"

"Can I come in? We need to talk," she said with her hand on her hip.

"Uhh... Yeah, come on in."

Savannah was stunned when she saw Erica sitting on the couch.

"Oh, wow. I didn't know you had company. We can talk some other time," she said with a look of disbelief written all over her face.

"Ain't no need for that. Erica was just about to leave," he replied.

"What you mean I'm 'bout to leave? I just got here. Why don't you tell that high yella bitch to come back another time!" Erica snapped.

Without warning, Bruno grabbed Erica by her hair, dragged her out the front door and threw her off the porch like a bag of trash. She hit the ground hard, laying there holding her neck and back in pain.

"Don't you ever talk to her like that! Now get the hell out of my yard, bitch!" he barked as he turned around and walked back inside the house.

Savannah was in the living room staring at him with her mouth open. She didn't know whether to feel flattered or horrified. This nigga was tripping. If she was smart, she would run away from him as fast as physically possible. But for some reason, her feet weren't moving.

"Have you had breakfast yet?" he asked.

"Breakfast? Are you crazy or something? You could go back to jail for what you just did to that girl."

"Here we go again." Bruno sighed as he walked in his bedroom and sat on the bed. "This conversation is boring."

Savannah was pissed. Who did this asshole think he was blowing her off like that? She stormed into the bedroom after him.

"I'm sorry if I'm boring you by telling you something that's going to keep your ignorant ass out of jail."

"Let me ask you something, Savannah. Why do you care what I do? You don't want nothing to do with me anyway."

"Are you serious? You don't know what I want. You've been gone for the last eight years. No phone calls, no letters, no nothing. You don't know anything about me. And the only reason I'm trying to help you is because I feel sorry for you. You're pathetic."

That hurt, but he didn't take the bait.

"That's what this is all about? You're mad because I didn't keep in contact with you? Savannah, I spent damn near my entire juvenile life in prison. While you were going to high school football games and pep rallies, I was watching Bloods, Crips, and Gangster Disciples stab the shit out of each other. I had to train my mind not to think about the free world. You don't think it hurt me having to live without you, my mama, and my sister? The only thing I could do to keep my sanity was to forget everything and everybody out here, but my feelings for you ain't never changed. How could they? I love you and I always have. We were meant to be together, and you know it. So, stop acting like you despise me when the truth is you want me so bad that I can have you whenever or however I want to," he said with his eyes locked onto hers.

She didn't see that coming. She felt her cheeks flame with embarrassment. She looked away, avoiding his gaze. "I don't know what you're talking about," she said in defiance.

"Yes, you do." He stood up from the bed and moved in so close to her that their bodies were pressed together. He rubbed his finger down her cheek. "You might not want to admit it, Savannah, but no one will ever love you like I do."

Her heart pounded inside of her chest. She wasn't afraid, but his eyes were dark and intense. His touch sent electrical sensations along her skin, down her jaw, up to the roots of her hair. Her breath strained and her body felt like it was on fire. Unable to control herself, she reached underneath his shirt and rubbed her hands across his chest. His body felt strong from all those years of fighting and lifting weights in prison. He pressed his hips into hers, backing her onto the bed. She felt herself responding to him. The only man she ever truly loved. He laid her down on her back, his mouth and body hard on hers. She was drawn to his intensity. She felt his nature straining inside of his jeans. Both of their eyes were drunk with lust. She knew he loved her, and she loved him also. He kissed her slowly and she gave herself to him completely without restraint. They sat up in the bed and slipped out of their clothes. He selfishly sucked her neck and shoulders. She traced the tattoos on his chest with the tip of her tongue.

"You're beautiful," he whispered in her ear. "Ain't nobody taking you away from me again."

He laid her down and penetrated her Garden of Eden. Her eyes flickered with pain. She saw the emotions burning in his eyes.

"I love you," he whispered. "I'll always love you."

"I love you too," she whispered back.

Nature took its course. Bruno was back in her life. He was back with a vengeance, claiming what was rightfully his, stroke by plunging stroke. She let out a strangled moan.

"Oh, Bruno! Oh, God! Oh, Bruno! Yes!" she screamed as the hands of fate swept them up, delivering them into blissful ecstasy.

About a half an hour later, she sat up. *That was amazing,* she thought to herself as she slowly slipped back into her clothes.

The ground was unsteady under her feet. Just looking at Bruno laying across the bed, chest soaked with sweat, made her want to go another round. Nobody had ever made her feel that way. She was hungry for more although she was uncomfortably aware that his mother and sister could return home at any minute. She was in love with him. She wanted him to move into her apartment so that they could make love all day, every day. But she wasn't thinking clearly. Too many emotions had surfaced that morning. She attempted to ignore them until she could deal with them practically, because they were too strong. He had literally taken control of her mind and body. I will not make a fool of myself over this man, she thought. However, she felt like she couldn't live without him. It was unsettling. She finally gave into her weakness. She kissed him gently on the lips.

"I want you to be my man," she said, eyes filled with icy flames. "And I want you to move in with me today."

Bruno smiled and kissed her slowly. A rooster crowed three times in the distance. The devil danced.

FIFTY-ONE

It was 3:34 AM

The air had cooled considerably with nightfall. Most everything was closed. There was an epidemic of after-hour criminal activity, the whores who walked the strip on the Boulevard, the crack spots, the back alley drugs deals and those who were addicted to riding those forbidden highs. The trap on Alexander Street had shut down for the night. Everybody had gone out that night to the club except for Red, his older sister Sandra, Jarvis, and that sexy little sixteen year old stripper he'd met the other night, Candace. Red was sound asleep on the living room couch. His hands were folded, at rest on his stomach, his mouth had dropped open, and his head tilted crazily to one side. Sandra was in the bedroom counting money and bagging up cocaine. She'd made a killing in Montgomery, but was ready to get back to Mobile because, as the saying goes, there's no place like home. As soon as they finished selling the last kilo that they had left, they were packing up and moving on. Jarvis was in the other bedroom with Candace, his underage entertainment for the night. Candace was a pimps wet dream. This girl was a petite chocolate sex machine, who brought meaning to the word fun sized. Jarvis had beat so deep into that sweet southern syrup that he didn't even have the energy to butter her pancakes, afterwards. She was well worth the two hundred dollars he paid her to stay with him for the night. She'd taken him past the point of ecstasy and beyond. Being as it was there wasn't any water or gas turned on in the house, Candace suggested that she walk around the corner to purchase some cigarettes, blunts, snacks and drinks from the twenty-four hour gas station. Jarvis didn't care. He gave her a twenty dollar bill and dozed off to sleep. It took her about ten minutes to make it to the gas station. She purchased a pack of Newport's, two boxes of Optimo blunts, some candy bars, and a two liter sprite. When she exited the store, she searched the parking lot until she found the car parked by the free air and water hoses. A silver 1987 Chevrolet Monte Carlo, that was in desperate need of some soap and water. She hopped in the backseat, a little nervous about being in the company of the Four Locos. Poncho was driving, Orlando on the passenger side, and Bruno and Mason in the backseat.

"What's it looking like?" Bruno asked her.

"It ain't but three people there, one of em is a girl and they all got long dreadlocks," she said, smacking on a piece of bubblegum. "And they got plenty of money, dope, and weed. They've been smoking blunts back-to-back since I've been there."

"What about guns?"

"Yeah, I saw some guns, but I don't know what kind they was."

"Where was everybody at when you left to come up here?" Bruno asked.

"Umm...The girl was in the bedroom. The guy I was with

was in another bedroom and there was a guy sleeping on the couch."

"Okay. You're doing real good. You ready to go back in and finish up?"

"Yup. Let's get this money, daddy," she said with a strong southern accent.

"Bet. We're gonna drop you off, down the street from the trap and you gon'-"

"I know," she interrupted. " know. Unlock the front and back door and when it pop off, I need to lay down on the floor 'til it's over."

"Yeah, you on point."

"And then I get my money?"

"Yeah, and then you get your money," Bruno promised.

They dropped Candace off then parked the Monte Carlo a few houses down from the trap, to avoid curious eyes. They popped the trunk to retrieve the necessary tools for the job. Orlando grabbed the Mossberg Combat 12 gauge. Bruno picked up the oowop, an uzi, stuffing it underneath his sweatshirt. Mason took the shotgun, a Remington Combat 870. He shoveled one of the shells into the shotgun and grabbed another one. Then he pumped the shotgun and chambered the first shell. Poncho stayed in the car with a Glock in his lap. His orders were to secure the scene outside. If anybody showed up at the trap while the Locos were inside, his job was to start murking motherfuckers. Everybody knew their roles, like gamblers shooting loaded dice, and they played them. Orlando and Bruno entered the front door while Mason crept through the back. Candace did exactly what she was supposed to do. So far, so good. The man Candace described was still asleep on the couch. From out of nowhere, he opens his eyes. When he saw the two masked men standing in front of him, he reached for his gun. Bruno squeezed the oowops' trigger, dumping five rounds into the middle of his face. Sandra, reacting to the gunshots coming from the living room, grabbed her Mack 10 from the bed, and started spraying like a terrorist. Rounds ate up the wall, chewing fat chunks of plaster and drywall and shitting them out on the floor. In the other bedroom, Jarvis picked up his .44 Magnum and started busting through the bedroom door. Candace jumped on the ground and crawled underneath the bed in fear. Bruno and Orlando took cover behind the couch, returning fire in the bedroom's direction. The inside of the tiny house had turned into a war zone. Everybody was shooting. A large cloud of plaster dust and gun smoke had filled the room, making it almost impossible to tell who was standing where. Sandra came running out of the bedroom screaming and spraying the Mack 10. The shots whizzed by Bruno and Orlando's head, blowing the far wall into pieces. Mason crept up out of the kitchen behind the enraged young woman, with his shotgun and pulled the trigger. The slug blew the life out of her, leaving a bloody mess all over the living room furniture. Jarvis continued firing from the other bedroom., leaving the door frame and half the surrounding wall ripped into splinters. Suddenly, his continuous fire stopped and it was replaced by a clicking sound. Jarvis was out of bullets. He immediately surrendered.

"I give up man! I give up!" He shouted. "Don't kill me. I got dope and money. Y'all can take it! It's all yours! I give up!"

"Throw that heat out the room and walk out slowly." Bruno told him.

Jarvis complied. When he walked out the room, Orlando hit him in the face with the butt of his 12 gauge. Jarvis hit the ground moaning and bleeding.

"Everybody aight?" Bruno asked.

Mason and Orlando nodded their heads. Orlando went and searched the rest of the trap, while Jarvis wept over the sight of his dead friends. Moments later, Orlando returned with a duffle bag filled with money and dope, and a scared Candace following close behind him.

"Finish it," Bruno ordered.

Jarvis was crying like a newborn baby, praying and begging to his higher power for help.

"Please, God. I don't want to die like this!" he cried.

Mason walked up and put the barrel of the shotgun to his head.

"Sorry. God's not home right now. Please leave a message at the beep. B-E-E-P," Mason said, mocking him. Then he pulled the trigger.

Candace screamed. The slug blew off his head and spray painted the room with blood. It was everywhere. Splattered across the walls and soaked into the carpet with a nasty reddish-brown stain. Bits of brain tissue stuck to the television screen along with mangled bodies torn up by bullets, twisted up on the floor. It was a room of horror. The Locos dropped their weapons inside of the trap and sprinted back to the Monte Carlo, dragging Candace along with them. Once they were all inside of the car, Poncho stepped on the gas pedal and faded off into the night ON their way back to the Southside, Candace was making Bruno nervous.

"You okay?" he asked. She nodded. Her face was deathly pale. She hadn't spoken a word since they'd left the trap. "What's up, Candace? You can tell me," Bruno said, wrapping his arm around her, holding her gently.

"It's just that I saw all those people alive one minute, and the next minute, they are dead. It was so much blood and death. I can't get their faces out of my head," she whispered.

"Calm down, baby. You gotta pull yourself together or you gon' get us all jammed up."

"I'm trying."

"Try harder."

She nodded.

Poncho gave Mason a look in the rearview mirror. They were cool for the moment, but it was only a matter of time before she flipped on them. Candace was going to be a problem. Bruno had an idea on how to handle it, and the sooner he took care of it, the better.

FIFTY-TWO

Tuscaloosa Fresh walked inside of this pool hall, "The Fresh Spot" on the Atlanta Highway.

He'd owned the place for five years now, and it was turning over a decent profit. However, the business' main purpose was to wash his dirty money. He was in a bad mood tonight because his lazy ass loud mouth wife had been complaining non stop, for the last six hours, about him not spending enough time at home. It was incredible to him how short her memory was. When they were living in that rat infested dump over in the Alberta community in Tuscaloosa, Alabama, she complained that his sorry good for nothing ass needed to get up, get out, and do something. No wonder so many black men were turning to interracial relationships, black women were impossible to please. Before he could even make it to the register to check his take for the night, his right-hand man and pool hall manager, Willie Black was signaling him from across the room.

"What's the problem?" Fresh asked.

"You got company, boss. In your office."

"Oh?" he said, surprised. "Who?"

"Larry O, and he don't seem happy."

"Well, what else is new?" Fresh replied. "Alright. Make sure I ain't disturbed until he leaves."

"I got you."

Tuscaloosa Fresh walked to the back of the pool hall and into his small office. Larry O was sitting in a chair in front of his desk.

"How's it going my friend?" he greeted as he sat in the comfortable leather chair, behind the desk. "What do I owe this unexpected visit?"

"Pour us up a couple of drinks. We gotta talk."

Fresh reached in the bottom drawer of his desk, pulling out a bottle of Jack Daniels and a couple of glasses. He poured two fingers into each glass and handed Larry a glass. Both men took a steady sip.

"So, what's going on?" Fresh asked.

"Have you been paying attention to what's playing out in front of you?"

"What's that supposed to mean?"

"What I mean is that there's a lot going on in the shadows with Big and his crew. If you watch closely, you'll see it. It's so obvious, it's unbelievable. That's how he's disguising it."

"Disguising what? You ain't making any sense."

"Our game. The game he's supposed to be playing. This ain't really about uniting the streets of Montgomery and sharing wealth with all sides of town. It's about his power and his money. Me, you, and Trick Shot are nothing but pawns. In the end, we gon' get screwed with no Vaseline," Larry said, eyes hot and furious.

"That's absurd! Where you hear that?"

"I didn't hear it from anywhere!" Larry snapped. "While you were growing up in Tuscaloosa, jumping around and cheering for your precious University of Alabama Roll Tide Football team, I was growing up on the streets of Montgomery, learning to see the shit before it hits the fan. I got a eye for this shit. I know what I see."

"For example?"

Larry took a sip of his whiskey and lit a cigar. "Aight. For example, Big's crew, the Locos, are putting down a nasty demonstration. They got the streets in panic, right now. Hell, there's like a couple hundred youngsters walking around out here claiming the Loco Gang. There's an army on the South-side and they're growing bigger and stronger every day. We ain't gonna be able to compete with them, if Big decides to turn on us. He knows that we're too smart to fall for his head games. That's why he made his move on Trick Shot."

"What was the move?" Fresh asked with concern in his voice.

"I'm glad you asked," Larry said, exhaling a cloud of cigar smoke in the air. "Everybody knows that them boys from Mobile was making a power move on the west side. They was bringing in their own product and killing the economy with their cheap prices. Trick Shot's crew was getting handled like some fuck boys by them outsiders. He never came to me or you for assistance. Next thing you know, the Mobile crew gets slumped. And I mean for real, it was a massacre. Folks are still talking about it on the streets, in the newspaper and on television. Trick's crew ain't built to apply pressure like that. The whole play has got Bruno and the Four Locos name written all over it. The streets is giving Trick Shot the credit for the demonstration. But Big knows that we can see through the smoke. All of this is a message to us."

"What's the message?"

"The message is that if we ever become a problem, he has the power and the killers to wipe us out."

Tuscaloosa Fresh steepled his hands, tapped his fingers against his chin.

"Are you sure about this?" he asked with a frown on his face.

"Wake up and smell the coffee, Fresh. Big ain't gonna piss on me and tell me it's raining."

"It makes sense," Fresh said, firing up a cigar. "That scene Bruno put on in Regency Park was a terrorist act. He's a low life thug with a powerful friend who has a steering wheel in his back. Well, I'm not some punk kid, fooled by his charismatic demeanor. I've seen him for what he is."

Larry shook his head. "I don't think any of us have seen him for what he is. Not yet."

"So, what do we do?"

"We play along for the time being. Big is the only one who knows the drug connect and he has connections inside of the police department. We gotta have all our ducks lined up before we make a move. There's a lot of money at stake and lives on the line. We have to be patient. I just need to know that you're with me when that door opens."

Fresh drained the rest of his drink.

"You have my support, Larry, but what about Trick?"

"Trick is weak. He'll ride with whoever has the upper hand, which will be us. After we touch Big and Bruno, we'll bury Trick wit 'em and ride off into the sunset richer than a motherfucker."

Both men stood up and shook hands.

"Remember to be patient," Larry said. "And we never had this conversation."

"Agreed," Fresh replied.

FIFTY-THREE

Bruno parked his truck beside Savannah's car then walked slowly upstairs to their apartment. His body was weary from hustling like a dog all day long with no regard for the law. He and Mason had been selling crack cocaine out of a seedy motel room from sunup till sundown without a break. They were work-a-holics who believed that long hours guaranteed success. Bruno was so happy when Poncho and Orlando showed up to relieve them that he barely said two words to anybody before he got in his truck and took off. He smelled something cooking when he walked inside his apartment, which immediately made his stomach growl. Savannah strolled out of the kitchen with a smile on her face, happy to see him. She was wearing winter white lounging pants with a white tank top. Her sandy brown hair had been gathered in a loose braid.

"Hey, Bruno." Standing on her toes, she pecked his lips with a quick kiss.

"What's up, baby girl. You lookin' good," he commented.

"Yeah, and you look tired," she replied.

"I am." He rubbed his fingers over his exhausted eyes. "I'm hungry too. What time we eatin'?"

"It's ready now. Go sit down at the table and I'll bring it out."

Bruno took a seat. He was anxious to see what Savannah had whipped up. He knew how talented she was in the kitchen, and he was hungry enough to eat a horse. She placed his food in front of him then sat in her chair across the table and blessed the food.

"Eat up," she said cheerfully.

"Fuck is this?" Bruno asked with a disgusted look on his face.

"Bruno!" Savannah snapped.

"I'm sorry, baby girl. Please excuse my French, but what the hell is this?"

"I made it in class today and everybody liked it," she said defensively. "It's a bowl of hot and sour soup and sautéed squid."

He looked at it like it was a big bowl of dog shit. "We must've run out of pork chops or something?" He frowned.

"Just try it, you jerk."

Wearily, Bruno picked up the spoon and sampled the creation. "Damn, this is pretty good, for real," he announced in shock.

"Good," Savannah said, relieved.

"You got skills for real, baby. You can make anything taste good."

"Yeah, I reckon." She grinned.

"So, how was cookin' school?" he asked while stuffing his mouth with squid.

"It was good. Mia was mad because our teacher, Chef Alexander, said I had the best dish in the class."

"Tell Mia to stop being a hater," Bruno joked. "You gon' be a Top Chef one day. Watch and see."

"And what are your goals, Bruno? I hope you got some other than what you are doing now. Only God knows what type of things you're mixed up in at the moment."

Bruno figured as long as he had bread coming in, who needed to work for a living.

"Yeah, I have major plans, baby, but they don't include working for nobody. I'ma own my own business or something. What do you think about that?"

"I think you'd be successful at whatever you put your mind to." Savannah smiled.

There's only the two of us, she reminded herself. And that's all she needed to be happy. It was all so normal eating dinner together at the end of the day, talking about how their day went, and their plans for the future. It's what she'd dreamed of her entire life. To simply be normal. Yeah, she wished Bruno would slow down and get a regular job but the likelihood of that happening fell into the snowball chance in hell category. But a girl could dream, couldn't she? Bruno got up from the table and walked over to where Savannah was contemplating.

"I have plans for right now," he said in a low raspy voice. "Are you interested?"

The question startled Savannah out of her silent thoughts.

"What are you talking about, Bruno?" she asked, chewing her bottom lip.

His eyes were smoky watching her mouth. He brushed his hand along the nape of her neck. At his touch, her desire leaped. Her skin was warm and silky, her hair caressed the back of his hand, and he completely felt overwhelmed with lustful urges. He'd taken off his shirt, and his dark skin glistened with a thin film of sweat. He scooped her up from the chair, cradling her in his powerful arms. The muscles of his back and shoulders flexed. He carried her into the bedroom and made love to her like their lives depended on it. When it was all said and done, Bruno snored between the sheets with an open mouth. Savannah pillowed her head on her hands and dozed off while basking in the aftermath of mind-blowing sex. Today was a good day.

FIFTY-FOUR

It was Kesha and Big's idea for the Four Locos to go out on a group date with their girlfriends. Big said it would be good for them to form a bond with each other's girlfriend, and for their girlfriends to form a bond with each other. Bruno didn't see the need for all of this, but whatever tune Big sang, Bruno danced along. That's how they all ended up at Moon Bar and Grill over in the Dalraida area. They'd ordered multiple pitchers of Miller Draft and the New Moon's signature southern fried chicken. The group finished off all the pitchers of beer before the food arrived, so, they decided to order more. Young people and alcohol, never a good combination.

"Okay, time for introductions," Shaelyn announced to the table. "I'm Shaelyn. I'm from the Vineyard. I work at the Walmart on Ann Street. I graduated from Jeff Davis High School. I love playing Scrabble in my spare time, and I'm super excited about getting to know all of you."

"We're super excited about getting to know you too," Mia replied with a warm smile. "I'm Mia, and that's my best friend,

Savannah. We're enrolled in the culinary arts program at Tren-holm Tech."

Samille, who'd had one too many glasses of beer, burst out laughing.

"What's so funny?" Mason asked, wanting to be in on the joke.

"I'm sorry," Samille said, still laughing. "It's just that the white girl has Mia talking all high class and proper. I like riding horseback through the forest and taking long walks on the beach. Bitch, please."

"Her name is Shaelyn," Mia said. "It's not that hard to remember."

"What?" Samille asked with a double dose of attitude.

"Shaelyn," Mia said again. "The white girl's name is Shaelyn."

"Which white girl are you talking about?"

"What's that supposed to mean?" Mia asked.

"It means that Shaeyln's white, and Savannah's basically white. So, I'm asking which white bitch you're referring to?" Samille said. "With your Samuel L. Jackson looking ass."

"Wow," Bruno said, shaking his head. "She's a real charmer, hood. What rock did you find her under?"

"Is that what time you on, Bruno?" Samille asked. "Are you really trying to go there?"

"Chill out, baby girl," Orlando told Samille. "Ain't no drama poppin' off in here tonight."

"Yeah," Mia warned her. "Chill out before the drama do get to poppin' off. I promise you don't want those problems." Samille fumed silently over Mia's smart-ass mouth.

The waiter brought out their platters of crispy fried southern chicken. The Four Locos began grabbing at pieces of fried bird like a ferocious fox snatching up big bone chickens inside of an unguarded hen house. Even though the men were devouring the chicken meat at a frantic pace, the women were able to salvage a couple of pieces from the Loco frenzy, and it was supremely good. In spite of that, there was still a hot cloud of hostility hanging in the air among them.

"The chicken was scrumptious," Shaelyn said, trying the conversation thingy again.

"Seasoned to perfection." Savannah smiled. "Whoever fried it was a master."

"We need some more alcohol," Orlando suggested, looking around for the waiter.

"So, now y'all the experts," Samille snorted. "Y'all should open up a chicken spot and call it Honky Chicks Chicken."

Orlando laughed hysterically. "Can I get a large glass of gluten free kool-aid to wash this Honky Chick ass chicken down with?" he joked.

Now he and Samille were both laughing uncontrollably.

"Bitch," Mia said. "You gotta fly ass mouth on you. Don't get slapped in it."

"She's drunk," Poncho told her. "Don't let her get under your skin, Mia."

"Orlando needs to put a muzzle on that dog ass bitch before he brings her out in public," Savannah added.

"Come on, ladies," Shaelyn pleaded. "We came out to have a good time. Can't we all get along?"

"It ain't work for Rodney King," Mia replied. "So don't hold your breath waiting for it now."

Bruno knew this whole group date experiment was a bad idea. Since the beginning of time, women have always been unapologetically vicious towards other women. Back in the prehistoric days, if a female couldn't lock down a male's attention, she was forced to live outside the cave with all the dinosaurs and homosexuals. It was a very traumatic environment to survive in. From that time forward, through centuries of evolution, women consider other women the enemy. They unknowingly associate other women with starvation and disease. Loyalty between women doesn't exist. At least that was Bruno's theory.

"Mia, all you do is run your mouth and talk shit," Samille pointed out.

"I can do that," Mia said. "God gave me a mouth, and I'm good at talking shit."

"Really?" Samille smirked. "I thought y'all Southside girls were good at sucking off dirty old men in the backseat of raggedy ass cars. Since ain't no men around, go ahead and suck on this, bitch." She picked up a chicken bone from her plate and slung it across the table at Mia, hitting her in the mouth.

Without thinking, Mia jumped up from her seat, grabbed a glass of warm beer off the table, and threw its contents in Samille's face.

"Oh my God!" Shaelyn shrieked. "What are y'all doing?"

Everyone at the table was in shock. What type of time were these crazy ass women on?

"That's yo' ass, bitch!" Samille hissed, standing up from the table with hell in her eyes.

Savannah immediately shot up from her seat and threw a right hook at Samille's jaw. Lucky for Samille, Bruno grabbed Savannah just in time, pulling her out of striking distance. If that punch would have landed, Samille might've had to eat her next meal through a straw.

"Stop it, Savannah," Bruno said, fighting to keep her restrained. The woman was like a mama bear protecting her cubs.

Orlando had his hands full trying to stop Samille from pulling out a razor blade she had stashed inside of her purse. Mason had to drag Mia out of the bar kicking and screaming. Shaelyn was looking at Poncho like *what the fuck?*

The entire date night episode turned into a Royal Rumble. Fortunately, everyone in the group made it out of the bar unharmed. Thank the good Lord for that tiny miracle. But believe me when I tell you the women all said a silent prayer that night for love, peace, and never having to see each other ever again.

FIFTY-FIVE

I t was a cold, rainy, dismal day. While normal citizens were inside of their warm homes with loved ones waiting for the weather to clear up, Candace was hiding out inside of a seedy motel room on the north side. It had been two weeks since she'd witnessed the most horrific acts of violence in her young, delinquent life. The shot-up bodies were everywhere, and she could still smell the overpowering odor of burnt gunpowder every time she took a breath. The Four Locos were a group of cash addicted thugs who could wet a young girl's panties by simply smiling at her. Ironically, behind those smiling faces were real life monsters who strong armed nightmares, twisting them unnaturally into heinous realities. Candace regretted the day she got mixed up with those trigger-happy psychopaths who murdered other young psychopaths with the ease and coldness of a Ghengis Khan led hit squad. What she needed to do was to get the hell up out of this God forsaken city as soon as possible. The only barrier in her way was a serious lack of funds. The money she'd earned for crossing out the Mobile hustlers had dwindled down to barely nothing. After paying for the motel room, a shitload of drugs, and a nice supply of alcohol, she was basically back to where she started. Maybe she could turn a couple tricks for a few dollars. Working the scene, she could easily scrape up enough money for a bus ticket to Birmingham.

There was no doubt in Candace's mind that the Four Locos were going to kill her. She'd witnessed a triple homicide. She could describe the actual crime scene in detail. She could identify each and every one of the shooters in court. That's what it all boiled down to. Candace was a loose string. Loose strings got cut. She had to figure out what her next move was going to be. The clock was ticking. But first, she needed to put some food in her stomach. The child hadn't eaten anything since the morning before. Even though the high life was a welcome escape, a girl couldn't live off Fentanyl and Wild Irish Rose alone. There was a McDonald's located a couple of blocks away from the motel. The sky was gray and soulless. After scanning her surroundings, to make sure there were no suspicious characters waiting in the shadows to drag her off into an unmarked grave, she headed towards her destination. The five minutes that it took to reach the McDonald's felt like the longest walk ever traveled. Every vehicle that drove by seemed suspicious. She entered the restaurant cautiously, eyes still scanning. The young employee working the cash register was annoyingly friendly, which amazingly calmed her nerves a bit. A Big Mac combo with a large coke and no ice.

She sat down at an empty booth, attacking the food like a starved animal. It was deliciously orgasmic. She dumped her trash in the bin and exited the building. Was she tripping? or was there a threat of danger in the air? Paranoia was a side effect of heavy drug use, so she figured that's where the feeling of imminent danger came from. The Four Locos probably weren't even looking for her. Yeah, she thought she was more than likely just being paranoid. It's amazing how common sense works better on a full stomach. For the first time since the massacre on the west side, Candace smiled. With closed eyes, she lifted her head to the sky to thank God for keeping her under his umbrella of protection. While thanking him for all his many blessings, someone tapped her shoulder from behind. She turned around, irritated by the interruption. After recognizing who it was, her blood went cold.

"Damn, Candace, you're a hard woman to catch up with." Poncho smiled. "Where have you been hiding?"

"I... I wasn't hiding," she stammered. "I was just-"

"It don't matter," he said in a smooth voice. "Let's get outta here. We need to talk." He grabbed her by the arm and led her over to where his truck was parked. "This is me right here." He opened the passenger side door for her. "Your chariot awaits, my lady."

"I... I got somewhere to be," she said, desperately trying to save her own life.

"It's raining out here," he told her. "Get in the truck. I'll take you where you need to go."

"I... My friends are coming to pick me up," she tried again. "They'll be here any minute."

"Candace," he flared without the smooth voice or fake smile. "Get in the fuckin' truck."

She unwillingly did what she was told. Poncho slammed the door behind her then walked around to the other side of the truck and sat in the driver's seat.

"Buckle up, it's the law," he said dryly.

The rapper Baby Gas' song "Street Vendor" played on the stereo as they pulled out of the McDonald's parking lot and into the flow of traffic.

"Where are we going?" Candace asked timidly.

Poncho ignored her, keeping his eyes focused on the road as he switched in and out of lanes. The debilitating fear that ate away at her soul grew stronger. She tried to fire up a Newport, but her tiny fingers were trembling so bad she couldn't even operate her pink Bic lighter. Giving up on the idea of a much-needed nicotine fix, she prayed a silent prayer. If this was going to be her last day on earth, she wanted God to know that she was sorry for all her many sins.

"I don't wanna die," she whispered with tears falling from her eyes.

Poncho acted as if she hadn't said anything at all. His silent attitude alone made it crystal clear what her fate was that day. The rain continued to pour. Whoever said life wasn't fair knew exactly what they were talking about.

Candace was only sixteen years old, basically still a baby in most decent folks' minds. During her short sixteen years on this planet, she'd been a whore, thief, gold digger, and strung out junkie who nobody cared about or loved. She was destined for failure from the very beginning. Poncho stopped at the red light. He looked at her with cold, calculated eyes. The eyes of a monster. It was the first time he'd looked at her since they'd left McDonald's parking lot. His stone-faced expression caused the tears falling from her eyes to pick up the pace.

"So," he said, in a calm voice. "Who you been talkin' to?"

Candace rolled her eyes and looked out the passenger window as if Poncho hadn't said anything.

"I'ma ask you one last time," he threatened her. "Who did you tell about our business on the Westside?"

"I didn't fuckin' tell nobody!" she snapped. "If anybody said something about that night, you might wanna go check your homeboys 'cause I ain't said shit! I know how to keep secrets. I been doin' it all my life."

"I was always told the only way three people can keep a secret is if two of them are dead."

The light turned green. Poncho went back to being silent as he pulled off from the traffic light. It was official. Candace thought she was definitely going to die. He drove another fifteen minutes before pulling over into an unimpressive looking parking lot. Candace instantly began to panic.

"You wanna know something?" Poncho said without emotion. "The majority of my brothers voted to have you touched. They think you're a liability. They don't know if you gon' roll over on us or not. They'd rather be safe than sorry."

"That's bullshit!" Candace cried, bursting into sobs. "Y'all came to me for help! I did what y'all told me to do, and now I gotta die!"

"That's just the way it goes when you're dealing with a bunch of paranoid gangsters."

He reached underneath his shirt. It's as if everything was moving in slow motion. Candace braced herself for a murder weapon that she was positive would be aimed at her head, but Poncho didn't pull out a gun. Instead, he pulled out a manilla envelope, dropping it into her lap.

"Lucky for you, Bruno doesn't think you'll roll over. He believes you're solid, and his vote is the only one that matters," he said.

Candace was shocked, thankful and relieved at the same time. She was going live. Thank you, Jesus.

"What's this?" she asked, picking up the envelope sitting in her lap.

"It's twenty racks and a bus ticket to Oklahoma City, Oklahoma."

"I don't understand," she said.

"This is how it's gon' work," he told her. "You gon' take that money and get on the bus, which leaves in about an hour."

That's when Candace realized they were parked in the Greyhound bus station parking lot.

"Oklahoma City!" She gasped once the reality of the situation set in. "I don't know nobody in Oklahoma."

"Do you know anybody in Greenwood Cemetery? 'Cause

that's where you goin' if you not on that bus. That's the deal. It's up to you," he countered.

"Well, I guess I'm going to Oklahoma," she said, quickly exiting the truck before Poncho changed his mind.

Candace was going to live to see another day, and that's what mattered in the end.

"Hey!" he called out to her before she could run inside the bus station. "You gotta second chance at life. Make the most of it, and don't ever come back to Alabama. Ain't no third chances. Not even for cute ride or die chicks."

She nodded her head, and Poncho sped off into the falling rain.

FIFTY-SIX

Bruno filled Big and Kesha in on what had popped off the other night at New Moon Bar and Grill. Big was troubled by the way the women behaved themselves. Kesha couldn't seem to stop herself from laughing. Those girls were just as loco as their boyfriends.

"It's funny now," Big said. "But what happens when that bad blood spreads and infects our entire family? If the Feds 'strategy is to divide and conquer, their work ain't gon' be difficult 'cause the Four Loco clan have already divided themselves."

Big's mind was made up. He was going to sit those hot-blooded young girls down and give them a good talking to. Their actions that night at the bar were unacceptable.

Which brings us to the present time...

The Four Locos, along with their better halves, were gathered in Big's backyard for Sunday dinner. This time, unlike the last, they were all on their best behavior. Big had a low tolerance for bullshit. So, any animosity or hard feelings were left at the front door. Kesha had requested that Savannah and Mia cook the meal. Excited about the chance to display their culinary art skills to the older woman, they happily agreed. The two best friends hooked up the night before at Savannah's apartment and put together a feast worthy of black royalty. Pickled oysters, stuffed pork chops served with lightly seasoned roasted asparagus and garlic mashed potatoes, avocado salad, and white chocolate pecan pie. The meal was a transcendent soul food experience. It was clear to everyone that Savannah and Mia were ridiculously talented inside the kitchen. Even though each savory dish was sinfully delicious and comforting nourishment for a sinner's soul, there was still somewhat of an ill feeling vibe suspended in the atmosphere. It was time for Big to intervene.

"Let me ask y'all something," he said, sitting at the head of the picnic table. "I don't want y'all to answer out loud, just think about the question. What kind of family do you come from?"

Everyone seated at the table looked at each other with silent questionable expressions on their faces. What kind of families did they come from? That was a peculiar question to ask. Where was the old man going with this?

"I don't know the details of your family situations or if you've ever dreamed of having a better one. But I do know y'all have a unique opportunity to be a part of something very special. Myself, Kesha, Bruno, Poncho, Orlando, and Mason have built an extremely functional family not related by blood. We support and love each other unconditionally. We can count on each other when our backs are against the wall. There's no reason for jealousy or envy between us. Each member of this family is important, and we want each other to succeed. My boys are all grown up now and have fallen in love with beautiful, intelligent women who I believe can add to this family and make it even stronger. I want you ladies to not just witness this unorthodox family of ours, but to imagine what it can be and how you can fit into it." He took a sip of liquor from his cup and lit his cigar. "I don't care about any petty ass beef y'all have with each other, or who started what. It's irrelevant. At the end of the day, we're family. When the chips are down and life starts throwing its trademark curve balls, it's the family that's gon' be there to aid and assist. The men y'all have fallen in love with are future kings, no doubt. So, the question you need to ask yourselves is are you disciplined enough to be with a King? And do you have the loyalty and perseverance to be a queen?"

There was a deafening silence around the picnic table as Big's words soaked into the women's minds. Family, that's what it was all about. Samille stood up from the table then made her way over to Mia.

"Look, sometimes when I drink, I can be a little obnoxious," she said sincerely. "I'm sorry, Mia."

"A little obnoxious?" Mia said, standing up. "It's all good, homegirl. It's water over the dam, or under the bridge, or whatever the hell the saying is."

Both women laughed

"Let me get in on some of that." Savannah said, walking over to give Samille and Mia a hug.

"Aww," Shaelyn cooed. "That's so sweet. Group hug everybody."

Everyone at the table laughed as the ill vibes evaporated from the atmosphere.

A little while later, everyone was scattered around the backyard in small groups. The women were huddled around Kesha on the patio as she bestowed a piece of advice.

"If you wanna be wifey then you gotta think like wifey," she was saying. "Start a family, keep your man happy, and always keep a savings account on the side to protect yourself if something happens to your man. This is life we're talking about, and in life, shit happens."

The younger women listened intently to every word that

flowed out of Kesha's mouth. because the older woman was dropping major jewels.

Big, Orlando, and Mason were talking football over the beer cooler.

"The Dallas Cowboys are hands down the best team in the NFL," Mason said.

"Ain't no way," Orlando replied. "You must ain't seen the Kansas City Chiefs play."

"They play next week in Kansas City," Big informed them.

"That's right," Mason said. "What you wanna bet on the game?"

"I dunno?" Orlando joked. "How about a hundred dollars and a shot of ass, you big country ass nigga."

Mason shot Orlando the finger. Big couldn't stop laughing,

Bruno was still seated at the picnic table with Poncho. The men shared a bottle of Pierre Ferrand Ancestrale Cognac.

"What up, hood?" Bruno said, taking a sip of Cognac and passing the bottle to Poncho. "What are you stressing over?"

"Who said I was stressed?" Poncho asked, taking a barbarian size gulp of liquor.

"Ain't nobody had to say nothing. It's written all over your face, homeboy."

Poncho looked at Bruno, then shook his head.

"It ain't nothing hood." He smiled. "I'm just stuck on what Big was saying about a queen. I think Shaelyn might be the one. I dunno, maybe. She's pretty, she has a big heart, and she loves herself some me. Sometimes I think she's too good to be true."

"You just scared, fool." Bruno laughed. "Shaelyn is perfect for you. If you don't put a baby in her and lock her down, you're a bigger pussy than I thought you were."

"That's easy for you to say." Poncho grinned.

"What?"

"You got your queen. You and Savannah have been stuck on each other since the days of Spiderman lunch boxes and

Tootsie Rolls. Who don't know that y'all sliding and riding till the wheels fall off?

Bruno glanced over at Savannah who was laughing with the other women over on the patio. *Damn, she is beautiful,* he thought. She was wearing a tight-fitting Juicy Couture sweat-suit, Chanel wedge heeled sandals on her feet, and a big leather Chanel bag slung over her shoulder. She turned her head slightly towards him and their eyes connected. Those gorgeous, bright, hazel eyes of hers sent a bolt of electricity through his body. As they stared at each other, reality hit him hard. Savannah was his soulmate. She was his queen. He had loved this resplendently beautiful woman for as far back as he could remember. He loved her to death...

To Be Continued...

Be sure to check out our other releases:
www.majorkeypublishing.com/novels

To submit a manuscript to be considered, email us at
submissions@majorkeypublishing.com

Be sure to LIKE our Major Key Publishing page on Facebook!

Made in United States
North Haven, CT
24 January 2024